BEN SMITH lives in Cornwall and is a lecturer in creative writing at Plymouth University, specializing in environmental literature and focusing particularly on oceans, climate change and the 'Anthropocene'. His first poetry pamphlet, *Sky Burials*, was published by Worple Press and his poetry and criticism have appeared in various journals and anthologies. *Doggerland* is his first novel.

Praise for *Doggerland*:

'Ben Smith has created a vision of the future in which the world ends with neither a bang nor a whimper but just rusts gradually into the sea. Ben Smith's writing is incredibly precise; working with a restricted palette of steel greys and flaking blues, he paints the boundaried seascape with vivid detail. This is a story about men and fathers, the faint consolation of routine, and the undying hope of finding out what lies beyond the horizon. I absolutely loved it'   JON MCGREGOR, author of *Reservoir 13*

'The novel belongs in a literary tradition of reflection on and solidarity with English nature, reaching back through Robert Macfarlane to Edward Thomas, Richard Jefferies and John Clare. It is a haunting story and could break the prejudice against speculative fiction often reflected in prize lists'

ALAN WARNER, *Guardian*

'These claustrophobic, contained lives are reminiscent of Beckett or perhaps Pinter ... An unremittingly wet book, damp and cold and rusted, blasted by waves and tempests, but also warm, generous and often genuinely moving. It is a debut of considerable force, emotional weight and technical acumen that weaves its own impressive course'   *Observer*

'Smith writes in controlled, lyrical prose, breaking up his narrative with elegantly expressed intercalary chapters'   *TLS*

'There's a patience and rhythm deep in the prose – this is going to make a mark'   CYNAN JONES, author of *The Dig*

'Trawled up from a new-old ocean, *Doggerland* reveals a drowned world, inundated by the past, haunted by the future. In terse, brilliant prose, Ben Smith evokes a terrible, stripped-down state. His book has all the urgent power of film – it might as well be set in outer space'

PHILIP HOARE, author of *RISINGTIDEFALLINGSTAR*

'An ecological horror which I read stricken and captivated from start to finish. Smith allows the enormity of the situation to dawn on us gradually and inexorably, scavenging what little hope remains along with our protagonists. *Doggerland* is a novel that holds its nerve, unflinchingly, combining minimalism with intense, lyrical flourishes. An astonishing, prophetic debut which should be read by everyone'

LUKE KENNARD, author of *The Transition*

'*Doggerland* is an astonishing work of fiction. As a reader, it's impossible not to be both awed and enthralled by the author's ability to sustain a page-turning drama at a physical location that to many is the epitome of nothingness … I was gripped from beginning to end. Every page exudes rust and salt, hope and love … it is the story of our times'

NICHOLAS CRANE, author of
The Making of the British Landscape

'Imagine, if you can, that Samuel Beckett, William Golding and J.G. Ballard got together to write a novel. It would be something like *Doggerland* – a melancholy yet riveting vision of isolation and endurance at the end of days. It heralds the arrival of a major talent'

GREGORY NORMINTON, author of *The Devil's Highway*

'The shade of Beckett hangs over this bleak, but haunting, tale characterised by a powerfully convincing relationship between two characters'   *Daily Mail*

Doggerland

Ben Smith

4th ESTATE · London

4th Estate
An imprint of HarperCollins*Publishers*
1 London Bridge Street
London SE1 9GF

www.4thEstate.co.uk

First published in Great Britain in 2019 by 4th Estate
This 4th Estate paperback edition published in 2020

1

Copyright © Ben Smith 2019

A catalogue record for this book is
available from the British Library

ISBN 978-0-00-831340-1

Set in Adobe Garamond Pro
Printed and bound in Great Britain by
CPI Group (UK) Ltd, Croydon

for Lucy

Bootlaces

Nothing. Nothing. Nothing. Something. Fourth hook down on the drop-line there was a dark shape. The boy stopped pulling and sat back on his heels. The swell was small that day and it was more than three metres from the platform down to the sea. The boy watched as the shape stretched and buckled beneath the grey water.

'Strange fish,' he said to no one.

The wind was blowing in from the west – consistent, ten or eleven metres per second by the feel of it – droning through the platform's pipes and grilles and pushing the sea into hard ridges. The North Sea shifted from horizon to horizon, like a tarpaulin being dragged over rough ground. It looked sluggish but, under the surface, currents ripped and surged. It was hard to imagine the sheer tonnages hauling past every minute, every second.

The boy wound the line around the railing until it was secure, then took hold of the hanging length, lifted it a few inches and let it fall. He moved it from side to side, but the hook was lodged. He'd have to pull it up. He moved the line again. It was heavy, whatever it was. He hoped his line wouldn't break. It had taken him a long time to get that length of cord. How long? Months? Years? He looked out at the horizon as if it would give him an answer, but couldn't even pick out where the grey of the sea became the grey of the sky. It was good cord. That was all that mattered. And a hundred miles offshore it wasn't easy to get hold of good cord.

Could you even get proper fishing line any more? The wind squalled and worked itself through the seams of his overalls. Who could he ask? The old man wouldn't know. He didn't know. And there was no one else out there.

He stood up, set his feet shoulder-width apart and pulled his sleeves down over his hands. He moved his hands slowly and kept the rest of his body very still, as if trying to steady himself against the motion of sea and sky. His legs were planted almost a metre apart and his sleeves barely covered his wide, calloused palms. Of course, the boy was not really a boy, any more than the old man was all that old; but names are relative, and out in the grey some kind of distinction was necessary.

He took hold of the line and, using the rail as a fulcrum, began to haul it up out of the water. As soon as the load broke the surface the line tightened and rasped through his sleeves. He stopped for a moment and let the wind smooth the edges of the pain, then carried on pulling until the fourth hook was level with the platform. He looked down over the rail.

It was a load of junk as usual – a greasy mass of netting and plastic, streaming and reeking. The whole thing was tangled into a dense lump, along with an oilcan, some polystyrene, and what looked like a burnt-out panel from a door.

The boy tied off the line, straightened his back and blew lightly on his palms. 'Good catch,' he said.

Beside him, the thick steel support rose twenty metres to the rig. Above the rig's squat rectangular housing, the blades of the nearest turbine turned slowly in the washed-out sky. All around, to every horizon, the blades of the wind farm turned.

The line spun slowly – ten turns one way, then a pause, then ten turns back. The boy lay down on his stomach, reached out and held the netting until it stilled.

The fields stretched out around him – row after row of turbines, like strange crops. From a distance, they all looked identical, but up close each tower was marked with dark blooms and scabs of rust. There were seepages of oil and grease creeping downward, streaks of salt corrosion reaching up, forming intricate patterns of stalactites and stalagmites. Some of the turbines had slumped down at an angle, their foundations crumbling like silt. Some had damaged blades and threw their remaining limbs around in jolting arcs. Others were missing their blades and nacelle entirely, leaving only the towers standing, like fingerposts marking the steady progression of malfunction and storm.

He tried to feel his way down to where his hook was caught. The net had floats and some kind of weights threaded through it, and it was twisted up with what could have been strips of weed but the boy knew were actually sheets of black plastic – he'd been finding them all over the farm recently. He worked his hand in and found the hook, then took a knife out of his pocket and began to cut away at the netting, strand by strand, until it slumped down into the water, leaving just the hook and the object it was stuck in.

It was a boot – black, Company issue, the same as the boy's. Except, where his were dark and supple from regular cleaning and waterproofing, this one was salt-stiffened, bleached and cracked, making it look like it was cut from some kind of rough stone.

He reached out slowly, tilted it and looked inside. The laces had come undone and it was empty, which was a relief. He'd found a boot once before, floating through the farm, still laced up tight. When was that? It had been down in the south fields. That boot had been brown, pointed at the toe. The leather and its contents had been scratched and picked apart. There must have been birds around then. And fish.

The boy put the knife away in his pocket and took out a battered digital watch. It was missing its strap and one button, and when he touched the display, bubbles of moisture spread inside the casing. It read quarter past five. He looked up at the sky and saw, perhaps, a paler patch of cloud in the west. When he closed his eyes the same patch appeared on the backs of his eyelids.

The wind dragged across the rig. Sometimes it sounded thin and hollow, sometimes it thudded as if it were a solid wall, impossible to move past. The line rocked. The turbines groaned and thrummed. The boy held the boot still. The sole was smooth and washed clean: the sea already cleaning things up, making things anonymous.

'Where have you come from?' he said. His voice was barely audible above the wind and the blades. Which was probably for the best, because it was a stupid question. And he was talking to a boot.

The currents that came through the farm swept in from the oceans and cycled round the whole North Sea, hauling waste and cast-offs out from every coastline. Some days there would be swathes of shining fluid that coated the surface of the water. Other days, shoals of plastic bags and bottles would rise from the depths like bulbous light-seeking creatures. The boy would find tidal barrages and bleached clothing, the brittle shells of electrical appliances. He'd seen furniture and timbers tangled together so they looked like makeshift rafts; and once, a whole house torn loose from its moorings, drifting through the farm, slumped and tilting on its flotation tanks.

Days, months and seasons passed through untethered and indistinct among the flotsam. Sometimes it felt colder and there were more storms, and sometimes a big spring tide would raise the water level up closer to the platform. But it was always cold, and there were always storms. It was spring now, according to the rig's computer. He looked down at his watch – it still read quarter past five.

He put it away and unhooked the boot carefully from his line. Then he got up off his stomach and sat on the platform, drawing his knees up against the wind and holding the boot in front of him. It could have come from anywhere. It could even have come from the farm. It could have been lost and then got stuck in one of the gyres that looped through the fields, catching anything that was adrift inside and not letting go. It could have been cycling round the turbines, round the edge of the rig, for years.

The boot was the same size as his own. Whoever it had belonged to would have been about his height, his build. The wind pressed in and the skin on his back tightened. What if …? But he didn't let himself finish the thought. There was no point going over all that.

He held the boot out over the water. If he let go, it could be gone in under a minute. In a day it could be out of the farm. In a few weeks it could wash up on the coast or, if it kept going, it could be pushed out north, up and over the pole.

Or maybe it wouldn't go anywhere. Maybe it would stay circling the fields. Maybe one day he would check his line and there it would be again – a bit more cracked, a bit more bleached, but the same old boot. And he would pull it up, unhook it and think the same old thoughts, ask the same old questions. And they would still be stupid questions. And he would still be talking to a boot.

He looked out at the water and twisted the boot's lace around his fingers. It was crusted with salt and had kinks from where it had been knotted. Slowly, he unpicked it from the stiff eyelets, coiled it and put it in his pocket. Then he reached out and dropped the boot over the edge of the platform. He watched as it dipped in the swell, pausing for a moment as if remembering its route, before drifting off east and into the grey.

'Ahoy there, Cap'n Cod.' The old man, Greil, spoke from where he was slumped in his chair. He had his feet up next to the bank of monitors and didn't bother turning round. The boy had been trying to walk quietly past the control room, but now stopped in the doorway. 'Why are you sneaking about?' the old man said.

The boy didn't answer.

'I saw you.' The old man inclined a foot towards one of the monitors. 'I see all from my eyrie. I am omniscient.' A hand appeared in emphasis, holding an enamel mug, in which sloshed a brutal-smelling ichor.

'What's that?' the boy said, stepping into the room.

'My finest. Not for your unrefined palate. Not since your last criticisms.' The old man swivelled his chair round. His cheeks were flushed purplish grey, like metal discoloured by a flame. His hands, clamped round the mug, had deep creases cross-hatching the knuckles.

There was no telling how old the old man actually was. His hair was still dark and slicked back into a hard shell, like the paint they used on the outside of the rig to stave off corrosion. Instead it was his eyes that seemed to have lost their colour. The boy was sure they had once been blue, but, like everything else on the farm, they seemed to have become bleached through years of exposure. He was small – much smaller than the boy –

7

but moved as if carrying a much greater bulk, always banging his elbows and knees in spaces that the boy moved through comfortably. At that moment, sitting still, he almost looked frail, until he leaned forward and stretched his neck, listening for the pop of each vertebra.

'And what bounteous harvest are you not sharing today?' he said.

The boy took the bootlace out of his pocket and held it up. There was an oil-stain on the back of his hand that looked like a broken ladder, or a broken yaw system, or maybe a broken piece of pipework. Something broken anyway. 'It's Company issue,' he said.

'Company issue.' The old man sighed. 'Well of course it's Company issue.' He lifted his foot. 'What kind of laces are on my boots?' He paused for the boy to answer, but there was no point answering. 'What kind of laces are on your boots?' He paused again. 'And what kind of laces are on the boots of every single person who has any business being in or around this entire sea?' All the while he was staring at the boy. The old man could stare for minutes without blinking – it was one of his 'people skills'.

The boy looked past the old man to the bank of monitors. There was the rig – all its corridors and crevices, like the twists on a circuit board. The screens switched from room to room. The galley with its long, steel table that could seat twenty – its cupboards stuffed with unused pans, cutlery and cooking utensils. On the work surface there were two empty tins; in the sink, two bowls, two forks and a blunted tin opener. Then the empty dormitories, the vast 'conference space', and the rec room with its listing pool table and the rig's only window – narrow and abraded with salt – stretching across the far wall.

The monitors flickered down to the transformer housing, which took up an entire level of the rig; the pipes of the old man's makeshift distillery snaking away into the dark. And down again to the dock, with its heavy gates enclosing a pool of still water. The dock was empty except for the maintenance boat, which was hoisted onto the slipway at the far end, charging off the main supply.

The screens shifted to the cameras on the rig's service platforms – the images grainy as dry putty. There had been a camera on the roof, but, like the buckled helipad and most of the aerials, antennae and satellite dishes, it was now defunct.

And beyond the rig to the fields – over six thousand turbines grouped into huge arrays. There was no stretch of horizon that wasn't planted, no hint of an edge or space beyond the churned air. In every image there was at least one turbine standing still and broken against the movement. At that moment, there were at least eight hundred and fifty of them scattered all over the farm. And more that were malfunctioning. It was hard to be sure, but the boy tried to keep track – it was their job to fix them.

Not that there was much they could do. With the tools and spare parts available they could only make surface repairs – replace the smaller gear wheels, weld, grease, rewire. More and more often, the only option they had was to shut the turbine down, feather the blades, apply the brake and leave it to rust.

The farm was running at fifty-nine per cent. Sometimes it was better, sometimes it was worse. Sometimes they would get spares on the quarterly supply boat, but more often they didn't. Sometimes the boy would pick a turbine and keep returning to it, on his own, until it was fixed. He'd once spent ten days going out to a single turbine, working through each component one by one. There had been something at almost every stage from control box to generator. When he'd finally got it functioning and checked the system, it turned out that the cable connecting the turbine to the grid had snapped somewhere along the seabed. Apparently, the old man had known about it for days, but hadn't wanted to spoil the boy's fun.

The screens moved from field to field. The images were in colour, but the sea came through in greyscale, slapping at the bases of the towers.

The old man looked from the boy to the bootlace and back to the boy. 'Good catch,' he said.

The boy watched the monitors. The sea slapped and slapped. 'Where do you reckon it came from?' he said.

The old man blinked. 'What?'

'The boot. The net was ...'

'What net?'

'It was tangled in a net.'

'You didn't say anything about a net.'

'It was just a net.'

'You didn't say anything about it.'

The boy folded the bootlace over in his palm. 'It was just a net. It had floats, weights tied in ...'

'Weights.' The old man chewed the word over, leaned back and took a sip from his mug. 'What kind of weights?'

'I don't know.'

'You didn't check?'

'No.'

'They were probably bricks.'

'They weren't the right shape.'

'But you didn't check.'

'No.'

The old man nodded slowly. 'They were probably bricks.'

The monitors switched from the galley to the rec room and back to the galley again. 'I'd never use bricks,' the old man said.

'Okay,' the boy said.

'Okay?' The old man leaned forward and tapped his finger against his temple. 'Think about it. Where would I find bricks out here?'

'I didn't say you would find bricks out here.'

'I *wouldn't* find bricks out here.'

'I know.'

'Exactly.' The old man raised his finger and swivelled his chair round to face the monitors again.

The boy could smell the salt from the bootlace, sticking to his skin. Salt had a very particular smell: sharp, metallic, but sometimes almost plant-like, as if it was alive rather than bits of mineral eroded from stone and dissolved in the sea. The old man swore it didn't smell, but to the boy it was everywhere, tangy and brackish. Either that, or he needed to wash better. He tried to remember the feeling of any other substance – sand, mud, soil – but all he could think of was the sole of the boot, scoured clean. 'It just made me think …'

The chair creaked as the old man swivelled it back round. 'Cogs,' he said.

'What?'

'Heavy ones. They make the best weights.'

The boy thought for a moment. 'That's what they were. Cogs.'

'What?'

'On the net. That's what they looked like.'

'What net?'

'The net,' the boy said. 'The one we were just talking about.'

The old man narrowed his eyes. 'You said they were bricks.'

'No, you said they were bricks.'

The old man reached under the desk and brought up a rectangular container with a small tap in one corner. He filled his mug. A smell somewhere between anti-rust and generator coolant swept over the room. 'How would I know what they were?' he said. 'I didn't even see them.'

One of the monitors showed nothing but the camera lens fogged with spray. The spray ran down and pooled in the corners of the screen, drip by drip by drip.

'It must have come from somewhere, though,' the boy said.

The old man held his mug halfway up to his mouth and watched the boy over the rim. 'Somewhere?' he said eventually.

'I mean …'

'It could have come from anywhere,' the old man said.

'Anywhere?'

'It's just klote.'

'I know, but …'

'It's just klote.'

'But don't you think …'

'Think!' The old man swung his hand in the direction of the monitors, slopping his drink over the desk. 'What good do you think *thinking* does?' He banged his mug down and began wiping the desk with his sleeve. 'It's just a boot. It's got bugger all to do with him.'

The boy's chest tightened. He stood very still, then raised his hand and rubbed the side of his jaw.

'And you look just like him when you do that,' the old man said.

The boy dropped his hand to his side. He could hear his heart thumping in his ears; or was that the waves, thumping deep down against the rig's supports? He put the lace in his pocket and stepped out into the corridor.

'Jem.'

The boy stopped, half-turned. They would go for months without using each other's names, so that, when they did, the words seemed random and unfixed, as if they could belong to anything – a tool or piece of machinery, or something that had just drifted through the farm.

'What are you going to do with your bootlace?' The old man spoke quietly. His eyes reflected the pale light of the monitors.

'Put another hook on my line.'

The old man raised his mug. 'Then we shall feast like kings on the fruits of the sea.' He drank, shuddered.

The boy waited in the doorway. 'Do you reckon there's anything down there?'

The old man leaned back and cradled his mug in both hands. 'There's plenty down there.'

'I meant …' But it was too late. Soon the old man would say 'a whole country, a whole continent'.

'A whole country, a whole continent.'

The boy pressed his forehead against the doorframe. 'Yeah, I know.'

'Right here, just below us. Thousands of years ago, all this was land.'

'I know.'

The old man closed his eyes. 'Riverbeds, forests, open plains. Villages, fire-pits …'

The boy walked down the corridor until the old man's voice was swallowed by the rig's own creaks and mutterings.

He stood below the clock on the wall of his room – it read midday, or midnight. The ticking echoed in the still and empty space. He took his watch out of his pocket. He'd just cleaned the battery connectors and the display now read '3.30'.

The dots between the numbers flashed with each passing second. He watched them closely, looking out for any glitch, for any slowing of the mechanism; but the beats were steady and even. He watched for a minute exactly, then took a tiny screwdriver from his pocket and inserted it into a hole in the backplate. The display changed to '0.00'.

14

He sat down on his bunk, which was, like everything else in his room, bolted to the wall and made of grey painted metal. *His* room, although there was little to show for it. There was a ten-litre container of cleaning fluid under the sink – the sort used for de-greasing gears and scouring the deck of the boat. Next to it was a bucket and cloth. The only colour came from the faded spines of three warped and torn technical manuals, which were stacked in the alcove beneath the bedside unit. Other than that, the room was the same as the day he'd arrived on the farm.

He remembered following the old man through the corridors up from the dock. The smell of grease and rust. The sound of the ventilators. The hollow sound of his boots on metal. The old man had led him to his room and they had stood there in silence, the boy by the bed, the old man in the doorway, both looking down at the small pile of belongings that the boy had brought with him: his Company-issue clothes, his Company-issue kit, his Company-issue watch. The old man had cleared his throat, gestured to the sink, the cupboard, the drawers, then cleared his throat again. The boy had stared down at the folds in his high-vis jacket, his overalls. Each fold was sharp and precise. When he'd finally looked up, the old man had gone.

The boy had lain down on the mattress and stared at the ceiling. It looked like it was rocking. It pitched and rocked and he'd closed his eyes, almost thought he heard the old man coming back, his step outside the door. But no one came in. The mattress had been hard and lumpy under his shoulders.

He remembered the particular way he'd had to curl up to sleep. Now it was smooth, worn-down, and fitted his body exactly.

Which was the only way of telling how long he'd been out there; how long he'd been fixing the turbines, setting out his fishing line, having the same conversations with the old man; how long since he'd been sent out to take over his father's contract.

Sometimes, he tried to think back to his life before the farm – even that first boat ride over, the last moments onshore – but his memories were hazy and indistinct, the way the turbines, in squally weather, would churn up so much spray that all edges and outlines disappeared.

He looked at his watch again. It was already a minute out of sync with the clock on the wall.

He got up and left the room, making his way down to the control room, stepping automatically over the loose floor panels, ducking under the botched and rerouted ventilation pipes and avoiding the third step on the stairwell, which was covered in a clear, glue-like substance. The old man had put it there, long ago, after the boy had tried to talk to him about keeping the rig clean. The idea was that the boy would get it on the soles of his boots and then it would be him treading dirty footprints all around the rig. This had never happened, but every few days the old man replenished the glue and every few days the boy avoided it. They both found it a boring and exhausting chore, but it filled the time.

The boy stood in the control-room doorway. 'What time is it?' he said.

The old man had his feet up on the desk. He shrugged. 'System's crashed again.'

'It did that this morning.'

'It's done it again.'

'Did you spill your drink on it?'

'I only did that once.' The processor chuntered and whined and the old man jabbed a button on the keyboard with his heel. 'Not my fault if it can't hold its liquor.'

The boy waited in the doorway while it reloaded. 'What time does it say?'

The old man sighed and twisted one of the monitors with his foot until it was facing him. 'Quarter past five.'

'Quarter past five?'

The old man shrugged again.

Nothing

The air in the tower was brackish and humid, the light the same strange yellow as a cloud before it dissolves into sleet.

The boy and the old man stood close, but not touching, in the turbine's small service lift, the toolbag propped between them. The old man pushed a button and they lurched up, rising in silence, or as close to silence as it ever got out in the fields. There was always the sea, the slow pulse of the blades and generators. And the wind, twisting its coarse fibres through everything.

They climbed higher and the noise increased. It was a hundred metres from jacket to nacelle and over that distance the wind speed grew until it forced itself in through every joint and rivet – between tower and nacelle, nacelle and hub, hub and spinner. All day, the boy would feel the thump of turbulence on metal, the vibrations making their way through his feet and hands into the cavities of his chest, until it seemed as though it was his own pulse knocking on the outer walls, wanting to come in.

'Thick slices of roast beef,' the old man said. 'Rare. With gravy.'

The boy looked at him. 'Rare?'

'Bloody.'

The boy counted the sections of the tower as they passed the joins. 'I know.' He always counted the sections, even though each tower was identical – made up of huge cylinders of metal, stacked like tins.

The lift doors opened and the boy picked up the toolbag and followed the old man out onto the gantry. They stopped at the bottom of a ladder and looked up at the hatch. It was rusted shut.

'Quiche,' the old man said. 'Cheese and onion quiche.' He'd been going on like this for over a week. The supply boat was late and they were running low on food.

The boy shrugged.

'What?' the old man said.

'I don't know.'

'You don't know what it is, or you don't know if you'd want to eat it?'

'What's the difference?' The boy put the bag down at the foot of the ladder and looked up at the scalloped rust.

Each day, the farm's automated system told them what jobs and repairs needed doing. There'd be a report through the computer on the rig, giving the turbine number, coordinates and details of the problem. The old technical manuals described the system as 'smart' – as well as controlling the direction the turbines faced, it could manage the output, slow the generators so they didn't overheat, and feather the blades if the wind was too strong. It was designed to let the operators know only if something broke, prioritizing the most serious cases, running diagnostics and even suggesting what tools to bring.

The boy often wondered if it had ever worked like that. After years of generating countless reports, the system was wrecked. It would say the problem was in a gearbox, when it was actually the yaw motor, or that the generator was faulty, when the blade controls were rusted out. Or it would send them to the wrong turbine completely and they would have to try and find out where the actual broken one might be – going round and round following the reports, like trying to follow the ramblings of a mind that was slowly unravelling.

This was the third job they'd tried to do that day. At the first turbine, there had been nothing wrong at all. At the second, the computer had identified a simple rewiring job; but when they'd arrived, the whole front of the nacelle had been missing – spinner, blades, everything – leaving a hole like a gaping mouth.

The boy took a drill out of the toolbag and searched around until he found a thick, worn bit, the thread ground down to smooth waves in the metal. He climbed up one rung of the ladder and got to work on the bolts in the rusted hinges. The drill jammed and cut out. He banged the battery pack against the ladder and it started up again. The bolts turned to a fine orange dust.

'What would you pick then?' the old man said. He leaned back against the handrail.

The boy reached for a pry bar. 'I don't know.' He could feel the old man's eyes at his back. Any moment he'd say something about the angle he was pushing at, or how the tip wasn't in the right place. 'I guess I'd pick that spicy stuff,' he said.

The old man closed his eyes and smiled. 'Pie crusts, yeah. Golden and crisp.'

'Crisp?'

'Of course. Got to be crisp.'

'How could it be crisp?'

'How *couldn't* it be crisp?'

'Because it comes in a tin.'

'Pie crusts in a tin?'

'Pie crusts?'

The old man breathed out heavily. 'What's the point in saying something if you don't know what it is?'

'I do know what it is.' The boy pushed harder against the pry bar. 'I just don't know what it's got to do with anything.'

'Then why did you say pie crusts?'

'I said *spicy stuff*.'

'Jesus.' The old man rubbed his forehead with his palm. 'You can't choose that.'

'Why not?'

'Because that would mean that out of anything – *anything* – that you could choose to arrive on the next supply boat, you'd choose spiced protein.'

Tins, dried goods and vacuum-packed blocks – this was all the food the supply boat ever brought. There would be chewy cubes of some kind of curd and packets of compressed rice.

21

The spiced protein was the only thing with any flavour, so it was always the first to go. They used it to bet with, and as payment for getting out of jobs they didn't want to do. The old man owed him four already. In the time leading up to the resupply, there would only be tinned vegetables left – gelatinous carbohydrates moulded into the shapes of things that once grew. They were pallid and starchy, and left a powdery residue that coated the tongue and teeth. With the boat being late, that was all they'd tasted for weeks. The only thing that gave the boy any solace was that the old man hated them even more than he did.

He pushed harder, but the pry bar slipped and he cracked his knuckles on the hatch. He dropped the pry bar in the bag, then clenched and unclenched his fists one by one.

'Could have told you that would happen,' the old man said.

The boy laid his palms flat against the hatch, braced against the lowest rung of the ladder and pushed the hatch up into the nacelle.

The old man went up first. No lights came on. Once, the boy had gone up into a nacelle and all the switches had been gently smouldering, molten plastic dripping down the walls like candle wax. There was a bang and muttered swearing, the flicking of buttons, then a screech of metal as the old man opened the roof hatch, letting in a shaft of daylight and a blast of sound.

The computer had said that the problem was with the generator, but when the boy climbed up he could see straight away that the generator was working fine. He blinked twice in the daylight, rubbed a hand over his eyes, then began checking each of the components.

There were a lot of ways that a turbine could go wrong. Mostly it was the weather getting in: crumbling seals on the hatches, loose rivets, scratches in the paintwork admitting the narrow end of a wedge of damp and corrosion. There were several different models on the farm and each had their own weaknesses – small differences that sprawled over time into repeated malfunctions or whole areas of the nacelle half-digested by rust. Some of the newer models were meant to be more resilient – better seals round the circuitry, fewer moving parts – but nothing stayed new or resilient for long.

The boy went over to the control panel, where a row of lights had gone out. He signalled to the old man, who sighed, opened the zip pocket at the front of his overalls and took out a decrepit tablet – two sides thick with tape and a crack in the corner of the screen, dark lines spreading across it like veins. The old man came over, plugged it into the control panel, tapped at the screen and then said something.

'What?' the boy shouted.

The old man cupped a hand over his ear. 'What?' he shouted back.

'I said "what",' the boy shouted, louder.

The old man stared at him for a moment, then put down the tablet and went to the front of the nacelle, removed the panel leading in to the rotor hub and crawled inside. After a few seconds, the blades slowed then stilled. The boy took out three LED lamps and positioned them round the nacelle, then

23

reached up and closed the roof hatch. For a moment, it was almost like silence. The old man backed out of the hub and returned to the tablet. He tapped at it again and nodded, which meant he didn't know what was wrong.

'What is it?' the boy said eventually.

The old man tapped at the tablet. 'Huài diào.'

'Huài diào?'

The old man shrugged.

'Which bit?'

The old man gestured towards the control panel. 'All of it.'

The boy took a step forward. 'Let me see.'

The old man unplugged the tablet and put it back in his pocket. 'No point. Don't know where the problem is. We'd need the control panel to tell us.'

The boy took a screwdriver out of his pocket and began to remove the casing of the control panel. 'I can work it out.'

The old man folded his arms. 'Waste of time.'

The boy removed the casing. Underneath there was a tangle of frayed and rusting circuitry.

'See,' the old man said.

The boy eased two wires apart with his screwdriver. Flakes of rust crumbled onto his hand.

'Got plenty to be getting on with,' the old man said. 'But if you want to spend all day playing electrician.' He leaned against the gearbox and closed his eyes.

The boy stood in front of the control panel. It was probably just a circuit board, or a few transistors. He could see what he needed to do with the wires. But if it wasn't, he'd end up there for hours and then they wouldn't have the right spares anyway. And it'd be another day wasted. A handful of electrical components. Everything else in the turbine was fine, but without the control panel the nacelle wouldn't be able to change direction, or the blades adjust their speed. A strong wind from the wrong direction and the whole hub could get torn off.

He shoved the screwdriver back into his pocket. 'Fine,' he said.

The old man opened one eye. 'What was that?'

The boy didn't reply. He just started unpacking the spare holdalls from the toolbag and they began to strip the nacelle.

Within half an hour they'd taken apart the generator and gearbox. The old man had removed anything useful from the rotor hub and packed it carefully in one of the bags. Then they unscrewed the panelling from the walls and bedplate, following lengths of copper wire, which they pulled out and wound into coils.

The boy took the first load down the lift and out to where the maintenance boat was moored to the jacket. The rain had set in, bleaching sharply from the west. He bowed his head to stop it hitting his eyes. This was how he thought of the weather: in terms of how much you had to bow. Sometimes he had to bend double, hauling himself along by railing and rung; sometimes it drove him to his knees.

He found some more bags in the cabin and sent them up in the lift, then waited at the foot of the tower. He could make so many repairs with the spare parts they'd just taken – they'd last for months, he could even go back and fix some of the turbines they'd had to shut down. But there was no point thinking like that. The old man kept all the parts so that he could trade for extras when the supply boat came.

The boy had only once questioned this, saying why couldn't they use some of the parts to make repairs?

'Why do you care?' the old man had said.

The boy had thought about it for a long time. About all the different ways the turbines seemed to groan; how a faulty motor would emit a small dry gasp just before it gave out; how plastic creaked like his own joints when he'd been kneeling in a spinner housing too long.

He hadn't been able to answer.

The boat moved slowly through the farm – a dark dot among the pale rows, rising and sinking as it cut through the swell. The boy sat in the open stern, his back braced against the cabin, watching the boat's wake spooling out behind them until it was pulled apart by the cross-currents, leaving no trace of their passage. Spray hissed against the deck and he looked up, then cursed under his breath. They should have been travelling south, but the boat had turned north, up into zone two. He knew because the corrosion on the towers was always worse on the south-west side – the metal blistered and peeling as if it had been subjected to flame.

He got up and opened the cabin door. The old man was standing at the wheel, squinting out of the cracked windscreen.

'How's the battery doing?' the boy said. He looked over at the gauge – the dial was about halfway. Out in the swell and chop of the fields it was impossible to know how long the battery would last. Cutting back against a strong current, it could drain fast. There were spares, but they were old and even more unreliable. There were times when they'd miscalculated and been forced to drift the boat, only using the engine to change direction. Once, when both spares were dead, their only option had been to moor up to a turbine and try to charge them off the main supply. Which the boy managed to do; but only after fusing one battery into a solid lump and being thrown twice against the tower's far wall.

'I'm running her slow,' the old man said.

'The gauge has been playing up.'

'I'm running her slow.'

The boy went in and closed the cabin door. 'How far's the next job?'

The old man didn't answer.

'There's four more turbines on the list.'

'It's been a good day's work.'

'We haven't fixed anything.'

The old man squinted out of the windscreen again. 'We've got what we need.'

The boy's face was stinging in the cabin's dry heat. 'We should at least try and fix one.'

'What if it needs parts?'

'It might not need parts.'

'But it *might* need parts.' The old man adjusted the wheel. 'And if we go fixing turbines with parts we've salvaged, we'll have to go around trying to find another turbine we can't fix, so we can get the parts back, all the while hoping we don't find one we *can* fix that will take another part that we've salvaged, which we'll then have to try and replace from somewhere else.'

'So we're not going to do any more work?'

'We can do some after,' the old man said. 'If there's time.'

The boy shook his head. There wouldn't be time. There was never time to do anything else when the old man took them off to check on his nets.

'Five,' the boy said. 'You owe me five tins now.'

The old man muttered that it was only four, it was definitely only four, but the boy had already gone back outside.

At any one time, the old man would have around a dozen nets scattered across the farm. If there was a system to their positioning, the boy could not fathom it. All he knew was that the old man spent days and nights studying tide charts and weather reports, making calculations, scrawling pages of notes and coordinates. The boy could almost have understood it, if the old man had been trying to catch fish.

But the old man wasn't fishing. He would string his nets between two turbines so they hung down to the seabed, then he would lower a twisted piece of turbine foundation from the stern of the boat and start to trawl: churning up the silt and clay, working loose whatever it was that he thought was down there.

He would talk about homes and settlements – a place that had flooded thousands of years ago. He would talk about woods and hills and rivers, and he would trade away crate-loads of turbine parts for maps that showed the seabed as if it were land, surveys from before the farm was built – the paper thin and flaky as rust – that described the density and make-up of the ground beneath the water. Every resupply he would trade for a new chart, or a new trawling tool, and then he would reposition his nets, rewrite his coordinates, and start the whole bloody process again.

The boat slowed. Up ahead there was a line of plastic bottles floating on the water. The old man piloted the boat in a wide arc towards the base of the nearest turbine, coming in slow until the scooped-out bow fitted round the curve of the jacket. The engine stopped and the old man came out on deck.

The boy went back into the cabin and lay on the floor. The boat swayed. The battery gauge hummed. The boy brought his hand up slowly and rubbed along his jaw.

Outside, the farm stretched away in every direction, the towers spreading out in rows, like the spokes of a wheel. Navigating through the farm, it sometimes felt like only the fields were moving. Whenever the boat turned, the towers would align along different vectors, and whenever the weather changed, the blades would shift position to face into the wind. There were whole zones that the boy had never even visited – fields well beyond the range of the boat's decrepit battery.

When the boy was out on his own he had to rely on the boat's satnav. He had tried to learn to use it less, but somehow he could never translate the satellite map's clean, segmented regions into the vastness of the farm. He had tried to talk to the old man about it, about how, wherever you were in the farm, it always felt like you were in the exact centre, like you could go on for ever and never find an edge against which to take a bearing. But the old man had just looked at him. 'Still using the satnav?' he'd said.

The boat rocked and shifted round the tower. Outside, the turbines started to move. The movement began on one horizon then spread like a ripple, as if a crowd of people, one by one, had noticed something and were silently turning to stare. The boy felt the old man step back down onto the boat, the scraping of the line against the side, then finally a series of heavy thuds as armfuls of net were hauled up onto the deck. As he worked, the old man hummed the strange tunes he sometimes hummed – mixed-up bits of adverts and songs for which the boy had no reference.

The sky turned brown and dim, like old water left sitting in a bucket. Soon, the last light would dip into the haze that always hung thick in the west. The boy got up and opened the cabin door.

Murky rain swathed everything. The old man was crouching down sorting through a pile of bottles, plastic bags, chunks of concrete and sludge-coated lumps. His hair was soaking and pools of rain gleamed in the creases of his coat. He hadn't even bothered to put his hood up. Eventually he stood, picked everything up and dumped it all over the side of the boat.

'Good catch,' the boy said, as the old man kicked the last shreds of plastic through the scuppers and back into the sea.

* * *

The boy read the instructions one more time. There was an open cookbook and a tin of re-formed vegetables on the counter, both stamped with a fading Company logo.

He put a frying pan on the nearest hotplate, opened the tin and emptied it into a bowl. Then he went to the crate in the corner of the room, where they kept all the empties, and found one that had contained protein mince. He wiped the inside with his finger and smeared the congealed fat on the surface of the pan, then turned on the heat. From the bowl, he selected the larger vegetables – orange discs, bulbous white and green florets – and added them to the pan. The fat was hot, but still congealed. It stuck to the vegetables in small white beads. The boy turned the heat up and pushed the vegetables around the pan with a spatula. They began to hiss and disintegrate, so he stopped moving them.

He watched the timer on the cooker and, after a minute exactly, added the other vegetables – small orbs and cubes – and left them popping in the pan. Then he turned back to the book. It said serve with potatoes. The boy didn't know what potatoes were. From the picture, they looked like the vacuum-packed starch blocks they sometimes got on the resupply. A gritty white powder that you boiled in water until it formed a thick paste. Little nutrition, but they made the tinned substances look more like food on the plate. He wished he'd saved one out.

He tried to stir the vegetables, but they had melted together into a grey disc and fused to the surface of the pan. He pushed at the blackened edge, but it was stuck. He turned off the heat, looked down at the picture of the meal in the book, then closed it slowly, picked up the pan and took it over to the table. He'd once tried to make something for him and the old man out of the book, and they'd both sat there for hours trying to finish it, until, finally, the old man had poured homebrew over their bowls and they'd downed them in one wincing gulp.

The book always said to 'season well'. The boy reached for the salt cellar but it was empty, so he got up and checked the cupboards. He saw himself for a moment, as if through one of the cameras, searching for salt in the middle of the sea. It'd be quicker if he just scraped some off his boots.

He opened the long, sliding door beneath the counter. The space behind was stuffed with pans that had never been used and instruction manuals for appliances that had long since broken. The boy squatted down and reached into the back – just more pans and empty packets, then a sharp edge. He pulled his hand out and saw a small cut on the tip of his finger. He rubbed the blood away then reached back in, took out the object and held it up to the light.

It looked like a turbine. It was only a few inches tall and it had been made by hand – cut and folded out of an empty tin. There were nicks along the edges that showed where the metal had been sheared. He took it over to the table and sat down, holding it up in front of him. He blew lightly and the blades turned.

The old man came in and crossed over to the cupboard. 'So I was thinking, seeing as you owe me five tins …' He stopped in the middle of the room and stared at the boy. 'Where did you get that?'

The boy turned the model round. It had been made very carefully. 'I just found it.'

'Give it here.' The old man's voice was low and quiet.

'It was in the cupboard.'

'Give it here.' The old man walked forward quickly and snatched it from the boy. 'I thought I'd got rid of all these.' He bent it in half and shoved it in his pocket.

The boy looked up at the old man. 'What is it?'

'Nothing.'

The water system groaned. The boy sat very still. His mouth felt suddenly dry. 'Did he …?'

'It's nothing,' the old man said again. He was about to say something else – his mouth moved, just a small twinge in the top corner, like a glitch between two wires – then he shook his head, turned and left the room.

Rain thumped against the rig. The boy didn't move. The cold metal of the stool pressed into the backs of his legs. The old man was right; it was nothing. He should just forget it. There were more important things to focus on. They'd lost another percentage of output since the morning, and there would be more turbines down tomorrow. The rain would work itself through rivets. Rust would bloom out of chipped paint.

It's not like there was much to forget anyway. One of the few clear memories he had was of the officials calling him in and asking him to sit down in one of their offices.

Unfortunate. That was what they'd said. It was unfortunate that his father had chosen to renege on his contract.

33

He couldn't remember who had spoken, or how many people were in that brightly lit room. All he could remember was that the veneer on the desk had been peeling away at one corner. He'd thought about what glue he would have used if he'd had to stick it back down.

They'd explained things very carefully. How the boy's position in the Company was affected. How the term of service had to be fulfilled and, as the only next of kin, this duty fell to him. It was unfortunate, they'd said, but it was policy. They went over the legal criteria and the job specifications, the duties and securities guaranteed. But they did not explain the one thing the boy most wanted to know.

'What does "renege" mean?' he'd once asked the old man, casually, in the middle of a job, like it was something he'd just read in one of his technical manuals.

The old man had looked at him for a long time out of the corner of his eye. His hand had moved to the ratchet in front of him, then stopped. 'Give up,' he'd said, finally.

Which was as much as he'd ever said on the subject. His face would darken and close over, as if a switch had clicked off. But it didn't matter. The more time the boy spent on the farm, the more he knew what it meant. It was something to do with the endlessness. It was something to do with the fact that there was no way out. The boy would stand on the edge of the rig's platform and look across the water. He knew, and he wanted to know, and he didn't want to know anything; like the waves churning between the towers, rearing up and splitting and knocking back into each other.

He looked down at his meal, which had hardened into a stiff mass. He touched it with his fork, then pushed the pan slowly off the table and into the bin. It didn't matter anyway. The food was packed with vitamins and supplements. A person could get by on less than a tin a day, and he'd already had vegetables for breakfast.

The water system groaned. The filters needed replacing and the water was already starting to taste brackish. It groaned again and the boy's stomach chimed in. He hit it with the flat of his hand. His meal smoked slowly in the bin.

Cracks

At night, when the boy couldn't sleep, he would take his tool-bag, his welding torch and a bucket of rustproof paint and go out into the corridors; making repairs, chasing draughts, trying to shore things up.

There. He would stop and put out his hand, then move it around slowly. There was always a draught somewhere. Up in the corners of the corridor, where the two wall plates met, or around the edges of the floor, the wind would be crawling through rivets, working its way through the cracks in the metal.

Outside, the weather would circle and press in. The wind would pitch itself low and sonorous, so that it sounded like voices speaking from every bolt and screw. Rain would echo off every surface. The boy would reach up and press his finger to the crack, feeling for the colder air. That was all there was – just a few sheets of corroding metal – separating him from the dark.

He would take out a tub of filler and get to work. He liked the way the filler smelled when it was damp – the gritty, chemical tang of it. He would lean close to the wall and breathe it in. Sometimes he would dip the pads of his fingers into the tub, wait for them to dry, then peel the curved pieces off one by one.

As he worked, he would recite from the technical manuals he kept in his room. 'There are several systems in place to prevent failures caused by adverse conditions.' He knew all three of the manuals by heart. 'The ride-through system prevents low-voltage disconnect by ...' Then something would start dripping somewhere up in the vents. He would tell himself that he'd checked them all recently and made sure they were sealed. It might just be condensation. If the dripping was regular then it was just condensation. He would stop and listen, measuring the sound against his heartbeat. It sounded regular. He breathed out. But what if his heart wasn't beating regularly? He would stop breathing and listen, and his wretched heart would begin an irregular beat.

The wind would knock against the rig and throw rain like punches.

'The ride-through system prevents ...'

The dripping would continue, each drop hitting the vent in exactly the same place, chipping away at the metal, molecule by molecule, millimetre by millimetre. Soon it would wear away a dent, then a divot, then a hole; then it would begin its work again on the layer below. Given time, a single drop of water would carve out a tunnel through every level of the rig.

The boy would reach for a screwdriver to open the vent but, just at that moment, the dripping would stop.

* * *

However much he tried to vary his route, to stay down in the dock or transformer housing, or keep to the upper levels, he always found himself working over to the washroom on the second floor. He would leave his tools by the door and cross the room to stand, in the dim light, staring at the mirror, which was tarnished and blotched with rust, except for two circles kept clean from years of polishing – one the right height for the old man and the other, almost a foot higher, which had stayed unused for years but now framed the boy's face exactly.

He would stand and stare into the mirror and think about the other things he'd found over the years. An oil-stained boot mark – too big for the old man, but almost the same size as the boy's – under the desk in the control room. A dusty set of overalls balled up on the floor of a wardrobe in one of the dormitories. A smudge on one of the pages in the cookbook that was there before the boy had first opened it. And, at the back of one of the cupboards in the galley, a bottle of strange green sauce that the old man hated, but had been almost empty when the boy arrived on the farm.

Then there were the things he'd noticed. The way that the old man would automatically pass him sweetener for his tea, even though he'd never used it in his life. How the old man would frown at the way he laid out his tools before a job. The way the old man would stare, when they were eating, when they were out on the boat, whenever he thought the boy wasn't watching.

The boy would lean forward towards his reflection and open his eyes wide. Had his skin always been that pale – almost grey?

The same grey as the walls and the floor. He would reach up and touch his cheek, his forehead, to make sure they had not in fact turned to metal. White moons would appear where he pressed his fingertips, and take a long time to fade.

There was just one meeting he could recall. A small room, rows of orange plastic chairs bolted to the floor, lining two walls. The boy had been sitting on one of them, his feet barely touching the floor. His father had been standing. The paint on the walls was flaking and there was a hairline crack running close to the boy's shoulder. He had traced his finger along it, over and over. He could still remember the course of the crack, the texture of the paint, the way the edges of it had bitten into his skin. He could remember his father's bulk, the creak of the new boots he'd been given ready for starting his contract, the sound one of the chairs had made when he eventually sat on it, but his face was as blurred and tarnished as the mirror.

His father's breath had been loud in the small room. It had smelled smoky, or maybe more like dust. He had knotted and unknotted a strap on the bag he was holding – he must have been leaving to go out to the farm that day. 'I'll get out,' he'd said. 'I'll come back for you, okay?' The boy remembered that; had always remembered it. And, for a time, he'd believed it too.

His hands would clench either side of the sink. Now here he was, instead.

For a moment, the wind would seem to drop and the rig would be quiet, almost silent. The lights would be low and seem to stretch for miles in the dark corridors. The corridors seemed to narrow and twist in on themselves, knotting the boy into the middle, the silence expanding and pressing in.

Then the wind would suddenly bawl, the air con would creak and whirr, the transformer would thrum from the floor below, and, deeper still, the waves would thud against the walls of the dock.

He was here to do the job. He just needed to focus on doing the job.

The boot-print didn't match his own exactly – it was wider at the toe, and the heel was not worn-down like his was. The overalls were dirty and frayed where the boy would have repaired them. And he'd once tried the green sauce, dipping the tip of his finger in and licking it, and it had burned his tongue.

The boy would step back, breathe on the mirror and wipe away the clean circle with his sleeve.

Sometimes, on his way back to his room, another sound would work its way up through the vents from somewhere inside the rig. It would begin with something rasping, which would turn to an uneven rattle, then a stutter, like an engine struggling to start. The boy would follow it along the corridors, up the stairs and into the sleeping quarters. Sometimes it would stop for a moment and he would pause and wait. But it always started up again.

He'd first heard it a few weeks after he'd arrived on the farm. He'd followed the sound into the galley, where he'd found the old man curled on the floor, coughing and spasming. The boy had almost shouted for help, then remembered where they were. So he'd done the only thing he could – gone back out into the corridor and waited until he'd heard the old man get up and begin to move around again.

He would take his watch out of his pocket and count the numbers. Sometimes it only lasted a couple of minutes; other times it went on for longer.

He would wait a minute. Then two.

After that first time, he'd expected the old man to say something, to tell him what was wrong. But the old man had never mentioned it, and the boy had never mentioned it, and so that was how it stood.

All the boy knew was that it was better when the weather was warmer, worse when the old man spent hours out in the wind and rain checking his nets. A mug of homebrew seemed to hold it off, but if the old man got drunk and fell asleep at the galley table, he would always wake up coughing.

After a while the boy had begun to see it as just another thing that happened: like the glitches in the computer system, the leaks in the vents, the cracks that spread endlessly through the rig, which the boy fixed only to find them creeping back again, almost too delicate to see.

Five minutes. Six.

Sometimes the sound turned harsher, more drawn-out. Sometimes the boy would take a slow breath in and picture the old man curled up on the floor, each cough ringing out like a radar blip with nothing to return the signal.

Seven.

He would breathe out, put his watch in his pocket and walk quickly towards the old man's room. But, just at that moment, the coughing would stop.

The boy would stand still and bend his head, listening. There would be no sound. Nothing would move. Then, from far off in the corridors, the dripping would start up again.

Junk

Field by field, row by row, the farm disappeared. First its outlines blurred and then it began to fade until blade was indistinguishable from tower, and tower from water, and water from the mist that settled over the sea. One by one, the cameras whited out, until the rig was completely cut off, like a component removed from a machine, then wrapped and packaged for transport.

The boy was in the control room early, working out the day's schedule. There was a lot of work to do. The farm had dropped another per cent in the last week, and the latest report was showing twenty turbines in zone three that had all gone down with exactly the same electrical fault. They needed to get over there and see what was going on, before the whole zone outed.

He was about to get up when he heard the clang of the dock gates. The screens shifted from white to white to white. He clicked on the camera in the dock and saw that the gates were open. Beyond them, the mist stood like a wall, then buckled and slumped inside like a sheet of insulation being unrolled.

The boy switched on the satellite map and scrolled across until he found the symbol for the maintenance boat. It was making its way out towards zone two. The boy sat back and shook his head. The old man had got the jump on him – piloting through the mist to check on his nets. There must have been some shift in the tides overnight, or a current had pushed in that the old man had somehow been aware of. He knew things like that – he could sense fluxes and storms as if he had a magnet inside him.

Once they'd been eating in the galley, when suddenly the old man had sat up and said, 'Something's going on out there.'

They'd gone to the rec room and looked out of the window and it had seemed, for a moment, as if all the turbines were floating in mid-air, a strip of sky underneath each one, the jackets surrounded by clouds instead of water.

The boy imagined the old man's blood prickling up like iron filings.

He would be out in the fields all day.

The boy got up and went out into the corridor. Then he came back and sat down again. The screen was still on the satellite map. It showed a pattern of bright green shapes against a background of vivid blue. However many times he looked at the map, he always had to take a moment to remind himself that those shapes were the churning, windswept fields and that static sheet of blue was the sea, rushing out there all around him.

This was the only map on the system and it showed nothing beyond the borders of the farm. The only signs of activity were a series of numbers next to each of the shapes, showing how many working turbines there were in the fields and the percentage of optimal output that each zone was running at. The specifics of corrosion, malfunction or weathering were invisible. The wind could be knocking on the shell of the rig, the waves sucking and tearing at the supports; but on the map everything would be static and silent. A wind farm with no wind, a sea with no currents or tides. The only record of a three-week storm would be a slight change in the numbers – all the damage of the wind and the waves, all those long, strung-out days and nights, reduced to a few altered digits.

The boy stared at the screen. The numbers flickered next to the shapes – two hundred and ninety-three turbines, fifty-five per cent; three hundred and seventeen turbines, forty-eight per cent; one hundred and two turbines, sixty-four per cent. The boy watched the numbers and tried not to think about how each percentage point would translate to hours working up in the nacelles, the days travelling across the farm, the spray flying across the deck, the cold splitting the skin on his knuckles as he tried to make repairs. How a whole day of work might add a percentage to the output, only for another thing to break and bring it back down again.

The boat's symbol was moving slowly into zone two. The boy switched the screen back to the cameras but could see nothing through the dripping mist. Once, when the old man had taken the boat out early and left him stuck on the rig all day, he'd found the camera on the nearest turbine to where the old man had moored, and brought it up on the screen. He'd waited for the old man to haul up his net, for him to crouch down and sift through whatever it was he'd got in there. But the old man had just stood on the edge of the boat and stared down into the water. The water had been dark and creased. He'd stood there and stared down and the boy had waited a long time, but the old man never moved.

The computer system whirred and groaned. Another turbine went down in zone three.

Later, the old man would bring the boat back with the battery drained and the boy would have to waste half the next morning charging it before he could get out to do any work.

The boat's symbol stopped. The old man must have moored up. He was probably standing out on deck right now, draped in mist, staring down, oblivious and unconcerned by all surface goings-on.

The boy sat in the galley and unpicked the last tangle of plastic from his line. He'd gone out to check on it, to pass some time, and found a huge shoal of bags that had drifted in overnight – a dark mass, silent and heavy, hanging in the fields as if they were waiting for something. Some of the bags had caught on his line and twisted it round the rig's support. He'd lost the bottom three hooks just pulling it up from the water. He held one of the frayed sidelines up to the light. Was that a bootlace? He sat and looked at it for a minute, then unpicked it from the main line. Whatever it was, it had become brittle and weak. He placed it on the desk alongside the swathes of wet plastic that covered the surface.

Most of the bags were so bleached that their original colours could only be seen in their creases and folds. Some were so heavily degraded that, when he touched them, they turned to brittle flakes that stuck to his hands. Others were tough and flexible, stained with colours that the boy didn't often see – red that was darker and richer than the warning signs on the rig; purple a bit like a bruise but lighter, more powdery; orange that was almost, but not quite, the same as the last of the flares he and the old man had let off, one by one, against the grey murk that hung over the farm for months without lifting. He picked up a green bag that still looked new, the logo and characters scrawled brightly down one side. He didn't recognize any of them. It had to be older than him. In his lifetime the only places to buy anything were the Company stores. The ownership changed hands, the management came and went, but still every bag carried their logo. It was easy to forget that there were things that existed before the Company took over; that even the farm had been built long before then.

He stared at the characters for so long that they blurred together. Sometimes he tried to imagine what the bags had once carried, what people had bought. Sometimes there were twists of polystyrene caught inside, or chunks of Styrofoam that must have calved off a bigger piece. He would try and fit the pieces together and work out what they used to be, how long they would have been drifting. But the polystyrene chipped off under his nails and the Styrofoam bent and tore, until there was no way of knowing what any of it had been.

Somewhere in the walls, the pipes let out a long, low groan. He unsnagged the last bag and pushed the sodden pile to the edge of the table. They dripped slowly onto the floor. He needed to do something. He stood up quickly. Hooks. He needed to make more hooks. He went back to the control room and unzipped his toolbag. The pliers had gone. He needed the pliers to make the hooks. He searched through the bag twice, then zipped it back up. The old man must have taken them again. The boy stayed still for a moment, then he turned and walked out of the room and down the corridor.

The door to the old man's room creaked softly. The boy opened it an inch at a time, until he heard it touch lightly against something. He squatted down, reached round and felt for the obstacle – a stack of four empty tins. He took hold of the bottom one and dragged the stack carefully across the tacky linoleum. As he pulled it round the edge of the door, he could see that the tins had been numbered and arranged with all but the third number facing into the room. All the doors to the sleeping quarters had locks, but the keycards were long lost, so the old man had developed his own elaborate precautions. The tins were an old system, but the numbers were new. The boy moved the stack out of the way, opened the door and stepped inside.

The room was laid out exactly the same as the boy's; the only difference was that here the furniture was barely visible.

The floor was a foot deep with twisted heaps of rusted metal, lumps of clay dried and cracking in pools of their own dust, piles of nets so stiff that, if you lifted them, they held their shape. A narrow path wound from the door to the bed, which was stacked with plastic crates. On top of the crates and spilling onto the floor were piles of paper – lists and tables, pages of scrawled notes and plans of the farm, all covered with indecipherable annotations, areas ticked and dotted and shaded with different-coloured pens. Some of the maps were old, from before the farm was built, and showed the seabed as if it were land – contour lines describing valleys and hills, a range of muted colours depicting the different rocks and minerals below the surface. The same red, yellow and black sediments streaked down the sides of the sink and made curved tide-lines on the floor beneath it. The sink was piled with half-cleaned objects, just beginning to appear from their shapeless crusts of mud and silt. It was just possible to make out slabs of water-blackened wood, bright stones and broken shells. Objects like these covered every surface of the room. They were stuffed into the chest of drawers and heaped in the open wardrobe and on top of the bedside unit.

The boy stepped slowly through the room, positioning his feet carefully on the narrow trail of clear floor. The edge of his boot caught on a pile of damp netting, dragging it greasily. He untangled himself and pushed the net back where it had been.

At first, it didn't seem like anyone even lived there. It was only after a few moments that small signs of human life became noticeable. There were two worn T-shirts and a pair of overalls slung over the end of the bed. Beneath these, the bed itself was unused – the sheets tucked in under the mattress and a single pillow, uncreased, at the head. Next to the bed there was a frayed woollen blanket strewn over a striped deckchair. All over the floor there were empty bottles of cleaning fluid and coolant that the old man used to store his homebrew, along with half-eaten tins of food discarded among the debris, forks and spoons standing stiff in them.

There was only one space in the room that was always clear and clean – a small semicircle on top of the chest of drawers, where miniature picks, chisels and pliers were laid like expensive cutlery. Today, there was something else there. The boy went over and looked at it. He knew it was a bone; but the bones he found in the old man's room were not like any he'd seen before he came to the farm. They were heavy, washed of colour and grainy to the touch – more like concrete than anything else. This one was a thick, squared ring, with ridges sticking out from its corners, almost like a cog. Which is what it was, really – a small part that had once made up a whole, a component taken from some lost machine.

The boy looked carefully at exactly where it had been left, then he picked it up. He wasn't sure if he'd seen it before or not. The disorder of the room made it hard to tell. It seemed as though the contents changed every few months, but that could have just been an effect of the accumulating variety of dirt.

He wondered if the old man knew where the bone had come from. Or if he even cared. Most of the things in his room seemed to serve no purpose at all. His drawers were full of pins, discs and flakes of stone – so thin they were almost trans-lucent – scratched with patterns of lines and dots. There were sharpened stone points, rocks worked into odd shapes, pebbles sanded down to accentuate their lumps and crevices. It had taken the boy a while to work out what they were meant to be – headless torsos with jutting breasts and smooth fat thighs that stirred strange thoughts he didn't know he possessed. He didn't look at them any more. If there ever had been a use for that stuff, there wasn't now.

All those years out with his nets and this was all the old man had to show for it – fragments of things that could never be fixed, never be put back together again.

That was all that would be left of the farm one day too. The towers and blades would degrade; the rig would crumble into the sea. When the whole farm finally got eaten away, the only things left would be its plastic parts – the latches and hooks, clips and cable-ties – all the small disposable components that were never designed to last, but would stay, like the teeth of some enormous sea creature, shed and forgotten throughout its life, becoming, in the end, the only record of its existence.

It'd happen even sooner if the old man kept wasting all of his time trawling up junk from the seabed.

The boy looked down at the bone again. He scratched his thumbnail against the rough surface, blew lightly across the hole, drawing out a quavering note, like a whistle.

Whistling. He heard it again. Working its way through the rig. Up from the loading bay. He looked around, but there were no clocks in the old man's room. He put the bone back

51

carefully where it had been, turned and moved quickly to the door, catching the stack of tins with his heel and scattering them across the floor. He dropped down onto his knees and felt around. There was the faint scrape of a crate being unloaded from the boat. He found three of the tins, but the last one had rolled in between the piles of netting. He searched as fast as he could, trying not to disturb anything. A tangled mass of rusted metal shifted and began to topple. He grabbed it and moved it back so it was balancing again. He found a tin, but this one was half-full of coagulated protein mince, which slipped in a thick disc onto his hand.

A cough. Loud and sharp. Then another. The boy stopped moving and held his breath. Silence. Then the scrape of the crate again, near the bottom of the stairs. The boy wiped his hand on his leg and fumbled through the piles of netting until he found the last tin, tangled. He tried to get to the edge of the net, but gave up and wrenched a hole in the brittle mesh.

He stacked the tins shakily, numbers facing the door, which he slid round and pulled almost shut. Once on the other side, he kneeled down and manoeuvred the tins slowly into position. At the last moment, he remembered to turn the third number to face into the room. Which he had to do blind, eyes closed, head down.

He pulled his arm free, realized he hadn't even looked for the pliers, closed the door and walked quickly along the corridor to his room. And winced as the stack of tins he'd built behind his own door crashed over and scattered across the floor.

c.8,200 Before Present

It ends with a wave. A single wave spreading across the horizon.
A neat crease in the surface of things. As it spreads, it grows in
height – ten feet, twenty feet, sixty feet. It hits a low island.
There is barely a pause. Just, perhaps, a slight adjustment in
direction and flow as the wave bends, folds, then passes on,
leaving behind nothing but open sea.

So, water completes its work – of levelling, of pressing in at
edges, of constantly seeking a return to an even surface, a steady
state. And now it is only the way the sea peaks and rises into
sudden, steep waves that hints at the landscape underneath – a
ridge that was once an island; an island that was once a coastline; a coastline that was once a range of hills at the heart of a
continent; a continent that was once frozen and covered over
by ice.

*

For a hundred thousand years the water waited, locked up as crystal, sheet and shelf. All was immobile, but for the slow formation of arc and icicle, which was the water remembering the waves it used to be and the waves it would become again. The only sound was the crackle of frozen mud and ice rind, which was the water, down to its very molecules, repeating its mantra: solidity is nothing but an interruption to continuous flow, an obstacle to be overcome, an imbalance to be rectified.

One hundred thousand years – barely worth mentioning in the lifetime of water.

All it needed was the slightest change in temperature. A few degrees and crystal unpicked itself from crystal, icebergs sheared – breccia to brash, floe to growler, old ice to slush. Each slippage building on the next, as the water reorganized itself and began to retrace its steps, probing at borders, undermining, working out the path of least resistance.

Until, somewhere to the north, a grain of thawing mud loosened from another grain of thawing mud, dislodging a coastal shelf, which caused a landslip, which caused the wave.

It is a simple history – of water turned to ice, returning to water. And, barely noticeable, somewhere in the middle of this cycle, plants and animals and people made this place their home.

A Fur Hat

The supply boat turned a slow arc and backed in. It was bigger than the service boat – deep-hulled and high-prowed for open water. The fenders thumped against the dock. There was no movement for a long time. Then, finally, the cabin door opened and the pilot appeared at the stern. He threw the ropes down and watched carefully as the knots were tied. His eyes were dim and sunken in the pale mass of his face, his head was shaved to a greenish grey and folds of freckled skin bunched at his collar and wrists, as if his bulk could not be contained by his neatly buttoned overalls. He clasped his small hands over his stomach as he waited. The boy passed him the charging cable. The pilot nodded, plugged the cable into a socket, then moved across the deck and lowered a gangplank down to where the old man was standing. He walked in short, careful steps, with his toes turned inwards, making it seem like he was constantly pitching forwards.

'I hope I'm not late,' he said. His voice was soft and clipped. 'Difficulties with the supply chain. Paperwork's been terrible.'

'I hadn't noticed,' the old man said. He turned to the boy. 'Had you noticed?'

'I hadn't noticed,' the boy said.

The pilot's face stayed smooth and impassive. Then he sighed quietly, took a remote control out of his pocket and opened a hatch in the middle of the deck. 'If you'd care to examine the goods.'

The hold was stacked with crates. Inside there were the usual tins and packages, identical vacuum-packed blocks. There was a small parcel of something like chewing gum, something less like chocolate, a bitter powdered green tea. One crate was filled entirely with spare water filters, another with coolant for the generators and one with a range of cleaning products in near-identical bottles – for use, as they saw fit, on the rig and on themselves.

The old man looked slowly through each crate, checking off the contents against some mental list of what he thought should be there. Inevitably, he would find something awry. He would say that he'd asked for new LEDs. The pilot would say he had not. The old man would say that he thought LEDs would be considered essential, integral to the good maintenance of the farm, and to be included on any shipment. The pilot would say he did not. The old man would ask whether the pilot would be able to do his work without enough LEDs. The pilot would say he could not, but that he always checked and made sure to ask for new LEDs when he was running low on spares. The old man would say that's why he *had* asked for them. The boy would sit on a crate in the corner and wait. They wouldn't even need LEDs.

After a while he got up and picked up a cardboard box he'd seen in one of the crates. He opened it and brought out a handful of red fabric.

'What the hell is that?' the old man said.

The pilot rubbed the corner of his eye with his little finger. 'Warm clothes. Like you've been asking for.'

'Like we've been asking for? You mean like we were asking for all winter and we've stopped asking for now that it's not winter?'

The pilot blinked. 'It gets too hot out here, does it?'

The boy reached further into the box and picked up a dark hat with earflaps. He rubbed the material between his finger and thumb. From a distance it looked black, but closer up it was deep brown, with strands the colour of rust. 'Is this real?' he said.

The pilot turned, took the hat from the boy and put it carefully back in the box. 'It's a real hat,' he said. He folded the box flaps closed, smoothing them down with the palms of his hands. When he let go, they sprung slowly back open.

'Have you got the stuff I actually asked for?' the old man said.

The boy reached in and touched the hat again. The material was dense and soft, but almost coarse, like there was grease in it deep down. He turned to the pilot. 'Where'd you get it?'

The pilot moistened his lips with the tip of his tongue.

The old man was standing with his arms folded, staring at the pilot. The pilot sighed again, went to the back of the hold and brought out another crate. The old man opened it and took out a pole, then another pole, then a series of further poles and attachments, which he proceeded to examine, one by one. Then he packed it all away again, nodded and picked up the crate.

'You asked for poles,' said the boy.

'Instruments,' said the old man.

'Let's call it apparatus,' said the pilot.

The boy closed the cardboard box and watched them leave the hold. 'Expensive poles,' he said.

They sat in the high-backed chairs around the table in the conference room. Between them was a pile of generator components, seeping grease and oil over the glass surface like the remains of some mechanical feast. The crate with the poles was next to the old man's chair. The pilot studied the components in front of him. 'And this is all yùnzhuăn?' he said eventually.

The old man nodded.

'Because if my clients find there's a piece missing …'

'"My clients". Jesus.'

'If they find …'

'It's all there.'

The old man had already given the pilot a full gearbox, two coils of copper wire and all of the individual parts they'd salvaged over the past months. Now he was handing over a generator.

'He can't take all that,' the boy thought; then realized he'd said it out loud.

The old man and the pilot both turned to look at him. The pilot picked up a section of the housing. 'It's all branded.' He spoke to the old man, but continued to look at the boy.

The old man shrugged as he turned back to the pilot. 'That's never bothered you before.'

'It bothers me now, though.' The pilot put down the component and folded his hands. They were very smooth and his nails were filed and clean. He was still looking at the boy. 'The parts are getting older. The profit margins are thinning.'

The boy looked down at the table. He could see the old man's reflection distorted in the sheen of grease. There were a hundred ways he could have used that generator. He could have split up the parts and fixed an entire row.

The old man picked up a length of copper wire and began twisting it round his hand. 'What do you want me to do about that?'

'Nothing, of course,' the pilot said. 'There's nothing that can be done.' He watched the old man winding and unwinding the wire.

The boy could smell the tarnished, bloody smell of the metal.

The old man sat back and smiled. 'Very philosophical.'

The pilot's eyes shifted back to the boy. 'Well, I suppose one must find some way of dealing with the pressures of offshore life.'

The old man was still smiling, but his jaw was tense. 'Can't say we've noticed.'

The pilot's eyes moved around the room, taking in the empty wall fittings, the buckled air vent and the turbine components piled in the corner. 'How's your hooch coming along, by the way?'

The old man stopped smiling. 'Do we have a deal?'

The pilot shifted position and let out a long breath through his nose. 'I'll be taking a risk,' he said. 'The margins, the pressures …'

'What do you know about pressures?' the boy said, too loudly. He suddenly felt too hot and the room seemed too small. The old man knew he wanted that generator. The boy had spent hours cleaning each component until they shone.

The old man frowned slightly and shook his head at the boy, but the boy didn't meet his eyes.

The pilot looked from the boy to the old man and back to the boy. He positioned a generator component carefully on the table in front of him. 'Nothing, I suppose,' he said. 'Compared to you.' He smiled slowly, then frowned, took a handkerchief out of his pocket and wiped the grease off his fingers. 'Although I could tell you some stories …'

The old man leaned forward. 'Do we have a deal or not?'

The pilot leaned back and folded his handkerchief, lining up the edges exactly. 'How *is* your hooch coming along?'

* * *

The pilot swayed and leaned back, balancing his bulk on the narrow stool. The shaft of which, bolted to the galley floor, creaked as he shifted his weight. He leaned further, until he reached a precarious angle. Then he crossed his ankles, reached for his mug, took another sip and coughed delicately.

'So, the brave and handsome pilot,' he said again. 'The hero of our story. He packed up his boat. Packed it up with everything.'

The boy was sitting at the other side of the table, staring down into his own, empty mug. The pilot had already told the story of the container girls and the one about the blind foreman and the whisky fog. Now he was on to a new one. He could slip from one story to the next without taking a breath, but once into it he would leave long pauses, waiting for his audience to respond.

'Everything?' the boy said eventually. His tongue felt hot and numb when he spoke. He'd already drunk three mugs of the old man's homebrew. Usually when the bottle was empty the pilot would leave, but the two-litre container was still over half-full. The edges of the boy's vision were starting to go cloudy and his palms were tingling. The effects of any two batches were never the same. One had caused his feet to swell up; another had made his chest itch for a week. He was sure he could hear ringing in his ears. But someone had to stay with the pilot, and the old man had taken his crate of poles and disappeared into his room about two hours ago. At least the boy didn't think he'd heard this story before.

The pilot nodded slowly and raised a finger. 'An excellent point. What do we mean by "everything"? To you, of course, it is …' he opened his hand and made a sweeping gesture towards the crates that were now stacked in the corner of the room '… such essential goods as I provide. Food, water-distillation systems …'

'Fur hats.'

The pilot looked at the boy. 'Exactly. He made sure he packed his fur hat.' He paused again and took a sip of his drink.

The boy breathed out heavily and rested his head on his hand.

'He packed everything neatly, took a complete inventory. Then he set off for the open sea …'

The old man came into the galley and began looking through the crates, unstacking each one and dragging them loudly across the floor. 'The open sea?' he said. 'What do you know about the open sea?'

The pilot blinked twice. His eyes were starting to go red around the rims. 'I've spent time offshore,' he said.

The old man carried on searching the crates. 'You mean your day trips?' He found whatever he was looking for, glanced at the boy, then left the room.

The pilot pursed his lips and watched him go. He pushed up one sleeve of his overalls and scratched his elbow, revealing a row of small, warped tattoos on his puckered skin. 'Well, we can't all be great adventurers, can we. With our maps and our nets.' He smoothed his sleeve back into place.

The boy waited, but the pilot kept on watching the empty doorway. 'His maps and his nets,' he said slowly.

'You were talking about the sea,' the boy said. The sooner the pilot finished his story, the sooner he might leave.

'Yes, I was, wasn't I? Well, he'd gone out a long way – out beyond the sight of land – when he noticed the boat was listing. He went down to the engine room and found a leak.'

There was definitely a ringing in the boy's ears. It was tinny and dull, like a bell buoy far out at sea.

'The boat was taking on water, the hold was fully stocked. Our brave pilot had to make a choice – try to make it back to land, knowing the boat would sink, or stay where he was and bail, knowing that all he could do was keep the water at bay until his strength gave out.' The pilot sat back and rested his mug on his stomach.

The boy stretched his jaw to try to stop the ringing, but the noise increased.

'I just thought you might find this an interesting conundrum,' the pilot said. He lifted his mug and took a sip. 'At what point does one decide to give up?'

The boy raised his head and the galley blurred. 'What did you say?'

The pilot swirled his drink. 'Just that it's easy to see how a person could let all this get to them.' He kept swirling, and the liquid rose up and grazed the rim of his mug.

The boy closed his eyes, trying to still the movement.

'The same struggle, day after day, year after year. The endlessness. I can only imagine how hard it must be, trying to keep this place going, knowing there's nothing you can really do.' The pilot leaned forward. His voice dropped. 'If you ever need anything. If you ever want to talk …'

'Talk?' The old man came back into the galley, picked up a mug from the side and sat down at the head of the table. 'We wouldn't want to put you out of a job.'

The pilot took a handkerchief out of his pocket and dabbed the corner of his mouth.

'Sorry.' The old man reached across the table and dragged t he bottle towards him. 'Have I interrupted one of your stories?'

The pilot folded a neat crease in his handkerchief and put it away in his pocket. 'Not quite. We were just discussing the importance of temperament.'

The old man filled his mug and took a long drink. His eyes slid across to the boy then back to the pilot. 'Temperament.'

'What it takes to deal with life out here. The necessary qualities for the job.'

The old man curled the corner of his mouth. 'Bad weather's coming in,' he said. 'We wouldn't want you getting caught in it.'

The ringing had turned to a dull throbbing behind the boy's eyes. He opened them, tried to focus on the old man and the pilot. They were sitting very still, but their outlines seemed to judder and blur, like an engine idling.

'It must be very useful,' the pilot continued. 'Being able to put everything to the back of your mind. What's your output these days? Sixty per cent?'

'Sixty-two,' the old man said.

'Fifty-seven,' the boy said.

The pilot's eyes flicked from the old man to the boy and back again. 'I admire it, I really do. The ability to compartmentalize. To shut things away and forget about them …'

The old man put his mug down on the table but still held it tightly. 'You don't know what you're talking about.'

'… to just carry on as you always have. With such certainty, such confidence. It really is—'

'You don't know what you're bloody talking about!' The old man slammed his mug down on the table, chipping off a flake of enamel that skidded across the surface.

As the boy watched, the old man's features seemed to shift and flatten, until the only distinction between him and the pilot was overall mass. All he could see clearly was the flake of white enamel on the table.

The pilot reached forward and lifted his mug, holding it protectively. 'This really is very good stuff. What did you say was in it again?'

The old man said nothing for a moment, then picked up the bottle and squinted at the faded label. 'Generator coolant.'

The pilot looked down at his mug, then gave a tight-lipped laugh – several short, sharp breaths through his nose. 'You should scale up your production. I know people who'd pay well for this.'

'Personal consumption only,' said the old man. 'For sharing with friends.'

'Tsjoch,' the pilot said, raising his mug. He reached for the bottle, filled his mug to the brim then sat back and took the smallest sip. 'Which reminds me …'

The boy stood up and left the room. The pilot had begun another story about a boatload of mealworms. He'd heard it before and the ending didn't make sense. He walked to the toilet at the end of the corridor and took a long, acrid piss in the scratched metal pan. The walls, the basin, the floor, were all dull grey steel. Sometimes, even on bitter nights, he would go out onto one of the service platforms just to take a piss and not hear the same metallic patter.

He breathed out slowly and splashed some water on his face. Then he walked back towards the galley. The pilot was still talking, so he crossed the corridor and went into the conference room. On the far side of the table there was the pile of kit the old man had given to the pilot. Enough parts to fix twenty turbines at least, and the generator in the middle. Traded away for a box of poles.

'Godverdomme,' the boy muttered.

'I know.' The old man was standing in the doorway. 'The end of that story doesn't even make sense.' He looked at the boy for a moment. 'He's finally said he's leaving. We could disconnect his bilge pump again.'

The boy glanced back at the turbine parts. 'If you want.'

The old man shrugged, then nodded towards the components. 'Get that lot packed up then. We don't want to keep him waiting.'

When the boy went back to the galley to find some empty crates, the pilot was leaning back and shaking his head. 'Don't make a meal out of it,' he said, gently wiping the corners of his eyes.

The boy stowed the last crate in the pilot's hold, then turned and sat down on top of it. His stomach was aching and he felt sick, but at least the ringing in his ears had stopped. As he sat in the dark, his head began to clear.

The pilot was still up in the rig. He'd got as far as the conference room, then started up with his views on the best distillation techniques – a last attempt to get the old man to slip his method.

The boat rocked as a large swell pressed in through the grilles beneath the dock gates. What had the pilot been talking about? Mealworms … fur hats … bailing something out? He shook his head, stood up and climbed the steps out of the hold.

As he passed the cabin, he noticed that the door was ajar. He stopped and listened – nothing but the quiet slapping of the water in the dock, the steady drone of the wind beyond the walls. He pushed the door slowly, then stood still and listened again. There were no voices, no footsteps on the stairs. He opened the door fully and went inside.

It didn't seem like the cabin of a boat. The floor was clean and shining, the surfaces free of dust and grease. Every dial on the control panel had been carefully polished. Against one wall, there were three locked filing cabinets, and a dark desk that looked like it might have been made out of wood. On the desk was a small pile of paper, arranged parallel to the edge, and a metal container holding six pencils, all sharp. Opposite the desk was a chest, on top of which was a large map, weighed down in all four corners by identical lead weights. The boy stepped quietly across to it.

It took him some time to work out what he was looking at. Then he realized it was a coastline. But where there had been a solid line separating land from water, the pilot had drawn in new, snaking contours marking the highs and lows of the tides. There were flood defences, drainage fields and reinforced beaches now well below the waterline. At the widened mouth of an estuary, a whole town had been given over to water, the limits of the daily tides carefully marked where they moved back and forth through its streets. Beyond the low-water mark the pilot had pencilled in the locations of a multitude of floating settlements and trading posts, makeshift rigs and marker buoys, annotating them with numbers and symbols in his precise hand. Pressed into the paper, there were also faint marks where other settlements had been erased. The boy leaned in closer and touched his thumb lightly against one of them.

He didn't know how long he had been standing there when he heard a noise behind him. For his size, the pilot moved quietly, stepping into the cabin and blocking the doorway.

The boy took his hand off the map. The edges of the land were scarred with inlets. He had a sudden memory of the feeling of crumbling earth, how it flaked away into water like rust off a corroding hull. He turned towards the door but the pilot stayed where he was.

'Don't worry,' the pilot said. 'It's good to have a healthy curiosity. Not to let yourself get too …' he raised his chin and glanced upwards, towards the rig '… insular.'

'I need to go.' The boy took a step, but still the pilot didn't move.

'I've got plenty of maps. The interior. The gas fields. The old cities. As I say, if there's ever anything you need. If you ever want to trade.'

The boy looked up at the pilot. 'You think I'm going to start stripping good turbines?'

The corner of the pilot's mouth twitched. 'I wouldn't ask you to do that. I know you've got more sense. But there are other things I'd be willing to consider.' He looked back towards the dock for a moment before carrying on. 'What is it, exactly, that the old man's been trawling up all these years?'

'What?'

'I assume he must be trawling for something. Not just digging holes in the seabed.'

'Why do you care?'

'Call it curiosity. I like to know what my associates are involved in. Then I know if the markets are …' he raised one hand then the other '… balanced.'

'It's just klote.'

The pilot nodded. 'Then I'm sure he wouldn't miss one or two items.'

The boy stepped forward again. 'I need to go.'

The pilot moved aside and folded his hands over his stomach as the boy walked past. 'Your father had a healthy curiosity too.'

The boy stopped. His chest tightened. He turned round slowly.

The pilot walked over to the map and began rolling it up. 'He was always asking questions – about the Company, the systems, the state of things onshore.' He glanced at the boy out of the corner of his eye. 'Never did trade with him. He didn't want to strip good turbines either. He was a good worker. Always fixing things. But then I'm sure the old man's told you all that before.'

The boy stood for a moment, in the middle of the cabin, then shook his head and carried on to the door. 'It doesn't matter now.'

'That sounds like the old man.' The pilot tapped both ends of the map on the wooden surface to straighten it, then placed it carefully in one of the drawers. 'And we know he isn't always the best judge of what matters, is he? Now, your father on the other hand …'

The boy stopped, but he didn't turn round. He heard the pilot moving across the cabin towards him. '… Your father saw the way things were going. He understood the pressures.' As the pilot came closer his voice grew even softer, until he was almost whispering. 'He really was a very good worker. It would have taken a lot to make him go off in that boat.'

The boy's chest tightened. 'What boat?'

The pilot was very close now. He had a smell that the boy didn't recognize, but he thought was probably soap. 'The other maintenance boat, of course.'

The boy looked out of the cabin window at the dock, the single charging bay. He shook his head and took another step towards the door.

'You didn't know that there were two?' the pilot said. 'There are always two boats. But you know what the batteries are like in those old things. It wouldn't have even got him out of the farm before …' The pilot breathed out slowly. 'But surely the old man told you this.'

The boy looked down at the floor. There was a scraping of something dark and gritty below the doorframe.

'I'm sorry,' the pilot said. 'I assumed you knew.'

The boy's chest was still too tight. He focused on the grit, on the way it had gathered along the line between the panels.

'I feel guilty,' said the pilot. 'I often wonder if I could have done more.' He sighed quietly. 'As I said before, if you ever need someone to talk to. Someone to trade with. I can get you anything you want.'

The boy stayed looking at the grit for a long while, then, finally, he made his legs work and stepped out of the cabin. The air was cold and he gulped it down. His stomach ached and his ears had started ringing again. A good worker. Another boat. The ringing got louder.

As he was crossing the dock, the pilot called to him and threw something down. The boy caught it. It was the fur hat.

'Anything you want,' the pilot said. 'Don't catch cold.'

Something

It had taken him an hour just to open the yaw casing. Another three to remove, clean and refit the bearings, working in the cramped space between the top of the tower and the nacelle's bedplate. His arms were aching and he could feel the first raw edge of a pulled muscle in his back.

He should have been able to get three or four turbines back online by now, but instead he'd been stuck up in this one all day. He'd known it was going to be a difficult job, as soon as he'd opened the casing and seen what a state it was in – it was packed with rust and everything was damp, even the rust was damp. But because he'd started he had to finish. Why did he always have to finish?

This was the first day since the resupply that he'd been able to get out and make repairs. Every other morning the old man had left the rig at dawn, travelled through the farm, moored up and taken out the poles the pilot had given him. He would carry them to the gunwale, then begin fixing them together and lowering them down into the water, adding more and more sections to increase their length. After a while – maybe when he reached the seabed – he would fix a T-bar to the top, turn it in slow circles, then begin the process of bringing the whole thing back up into the boat. He'd been performing this same ritual every day, all across the farm.

It was even worse than the nets. The old man would probably start trying to dive down there himself soon.

The boy jammed the last bearing into place, sat upright and stretched his back.

Outside it was starting to get dark – the sky yellowing at the edges, turning the colour of old smoke. The boy couldn't see this, but he knew it was happening from the change in the wind that often accompanied the dusk.

He stretched again and his ears popped. They'd been doing that on and off since he'd drunk all that homebrew the night of the resupply. He swore never to drink it again. At least not from that batch. If he hadn't drunk so much of it he would never have gone into the pilot's cabin, he would never have heard the klote the pilot said, or stayed there, listening.

He shook his head. A second boat. The pilot always made up good stories. He'd once, a long time ago, told the boy that all rigs were equipped with an emergency set of tools hidden under the floor panels and the boy had believed him, going as far as to lever up the entire first-floor corridor until the old man had fallen into one of the holes and said was the boy slackened? Why would anyone hide emergency tools? If there was a bloody emergency no one would have the time to pull up a bloody floor, would they? And if he didn't put the panels back right away he'd bury *him* under them.

The boy's face still burned when he thought about it.

He packed away his tools and closed up the yaw housing. He pushed the panel shut, but it swung back open. He pushed it shut again, and it swung back open. The latch had fallen off.

'Not now,' he said.

He pushed the panel shut, held it for a moment then released it gently. It swung back open.

'Don't do this now,' he said.

It was just one panel. One panel in a fully working turbine. He could just leave it and go. He breathed out slowly. One panel that would stay hanging open, swinging every time the nacelle turned and tapping in the mechanical breeze that came from the cooling system. Tapping and tapping for ever. He reached out and held it, even though it wasn't moving.

'Fine,' he said. 'Have it your bloody way.'

He took his watch out of his pocket. The time was wrong again, but he'd been using the stopwatch function to gauge his trip – he had maybe another hour of light.

Outside, on the eastern horizon, darkness would be spreading up from the water, until only the pale tops of the towers would be visible, like candles that were guttering and about to go out.

He put the watch away and reached into the housing to try to find the broken piece. He could glue it back together. Just enough for it to hold. Just enough so he could tell himself that he'd been able to finish the job.

His arm rubbed against the bearings and smeared grease up his sleeve. He closed his eyes and reached in further. In the bottom corner of the housing, he felt something. He picked it up and held it to the light. It was a latch, but it wasn't the original latch from the panel – they were black and mass-moulded. This one was hand-cut from a piece of blue plastic. It had a square hole at one end, so it could be fitted over the spindle and a hook cut into the other. The hook was cut deeper than on the standard latches, making a better connection with the receiver. It was a good repair – the sort of thing that the boy might have done.

There was no draught in the tower, but the skin tightened on the boy's arms and neck.

He was good at fixing things; that's what the pilot had said.

The boy sat on the bedplate, holding the latch gently in his palm, running his thumb over the edges. After a while, he pushed it back onto the broken spindle, then closed the panel, raising and lowering the handle carefully until he felt the hook catch.

The next day he didn't mind when he heard the old man go out at dawn. He went to the control room and sat in front of the screens. But he didn't look at the cameras, or even check the farm's output. Instead, he opened up the service-schedule archives and began scrolling through, until he reached the records of the maintenance reports that were generated before he arrived on the farm.

There was no way of telling if the work had been carried out. Like now, none of the reports were filled in or signed off. Like now, they were confused and sprawling. But they did give details of the scheduled repairs and the boy went through the reports slowly, noting down the locations of each one.

By the time the old man returned, the boy had gone back through almost a year of reports and noted the locations of all the repairs. He waited until the old man was in his room, then he took the boat out and entered the coordinates of the nearest one.

Most of the turbines revealed nothing, or they were too rusted out, too dangerous to venture up; but over the days and weeks there were some discoveries. He found handmade bearings so well crafted that they still ran smoothly; the most intricate rerouting of a wind sensor he'd ever seen; and, in a nacelle gaping with holes – its bedplate eaten away, its control panel caked in salt – he found a gearbox that had been serviced and perfectly sealed, all its inner workings still bright and clean.

He had a sudden memory of a ratchet he used to use when he'd first arrived on the farm. He'd found it at the back of the storeroom, and he'd liked using it because the handle was smooth and worn-down and fitted his hand exactly. He'd lost it in the south fields – a wave had jumped up over the gunwale and dragged it under – but he still remembered how well it had worked, the smoothness that moulded to the shape of his palm.

The boy continued to go through the old reports, plotting them on the satellite map, following their course through the farm. By day he would visit and revisit the same repairs, studying them closely. At night he would lie on his bed, working out exactly how they'd been made, what tools had been used, whether he would have done anything differently.

Then one day he was looking through an old schedule and he found a service record for the maintenance boat. He looked closer and saw that the file gave details of repairs on two boats.

The screen flickered in front of him. He sat back and closed his eyes, then opened them, leaned forward and checked the screen again. There were two different boats – each one had its own registration number.

The screen flickered again. His hands went very cold and he almost couldn't move them to type. He entered the registration number of the second boat into the system. A list flashed up. It took him a moment to focus clearly enough to read it. It was a list of repairs. The second boat had been allocated all of the repairs that he'd found. He sat back and looked at the screen for a long time. That was his father's boat.

The screen flickered again then cut out. All the screens went black and the system groaned then went silent. The boy jumped out of the chair. 'Shit,' he said. He hit the side of the screen. A blue light flashed up then faded. He turned the screen off then back on. Nothing. He went over to the main computer and hit that too. Then he turned off the isolator switch and rebooted everything.

It took a long time for the system to power back up. By the time it had the boy's hands were shaking. He leaned straight in and got to work. If he cross-referenced the old schedules with the boat's registration, he'd be able to find all of the repairs his father had ever made. He reached for the keyboard, then stopped. What if he checked the registration against the satellite map's archives?

He brought up the map and entered the numbers. The processors chuntered and whirred; the screen froze for a few seconds; then a fretwork of lines began to appear across the map, building, layering over one another into a tight mesh that covered the farm.

Here was a complete record of his father's movements – all the turbines and transformers he'd ever visited, every journey he'd taken through the farm. By following the densest patterns of lines, the boy could make out the routes he most often used, the rows he favoured, the fact that he always plotted his maintenance route in a clockwise direction, and that almost every day he would take a detour out to the western edge of the farm and follow its limit for miles before turning back to the rig.

The boy raced through the dates of each recorded journey – working through the months, the years – then he saw it, down in the south fields: the last record of the boat, at the moment its tracker had failed.

He sat very still and looked at the screen. That was it. That was where it had happened. Whatever it was exactly that had happened.

He took his watch out of his pocket and looked up at the cameras. His watch had stopped and the screens were almost dark. The old man had only just come back and the boat was only half-charged. Maybe he should wait. What good would it do rushing off into the night? He switched the screen back to the maintenance report. He should do some work. He should check his line. He should think about all of this carefully.

He reached for the keyboard, then pushed his chair back and stood up. If he didn't go now, he never would.

As he turned into the stairwell, he almost collided with the old man, who was making his way up from the transformer level with a fresh container of homebrew.

'You shouldn't run in the workplace,' the old man said.

The boy moved down a step.

'Where are you going?' the old man said.

'There's work that needs doing.'

'You should relax. Learn to enjoy things a bit.' The old man raised the container. 'I might even let you share this batch if you're lucky.'

'There's work that needs doing.'

'Do you remember the first time you tried this stuff?'

The boy put his hand on the railing and looked down the stairs.

'I wouldn't let you have any, so you sneaked into my distillery and drank it raw from the vat.' The old man laughed. 'I found you on your back in the corridor. Had to drag you to your bed, sit with you while you kept telling me about … what was it?'

'I don't remember,' the boy said. His thoughts were surging, he could barely hear what the old man was saying. The boat. All he could think about was the boat. The old man had never said a word about it.

'You must do. It was something about fish eating all the protein.'

'What?'

'The spiced protein.' The old man changed the container over to his other hand. 'I remember that you—'

'I don't remember,' the boy said.

The old man stopped. He nodded slowly and sighed.

The boy took another step down.

'Wait,' the old man said.

The boy stopped.

The old man just watched him. Then the corner of his mouth began to twitch. 'Have a good evening then,' he said and carried on up the stairs.

The boy breathed out heavily, then tried to carry on down to the dock. But his feet wouldn't move. He lost balance and had to grip the banister. He tried again, but his feet were stuck. He looked down and saw he was standing on the step that was always covered in glue.

The old man's laughter echoed through the corridors of the rig.

The boy unlaced his boots and left them where they were, then walked barefoot down to the storeroom to find a chisel.

* * *

Dusk spread across the sea, turning it slick and dark as oil. The boy made his way to the south fields, running the boat at full throttle. At some point a bank of clouds pushed in from the south-west and it began to rain, blurring the towers and reducing visibility to a couple of rows.

The battery gauge dropped, so he reduced his speed. He was close now. Just a few miles. He squinted out of the wind-screen through the brief gaps left by the wiper blades. The rain drummed on the cabin roof.

Soon the glow from the satnav screen grew brighter than the sky. The boy switched on the boat's headlights and continued on his course. He was nearing the place now. One hundred metres, fifty metres. The night crowded in. The rain cut down through the headlight beams, shortening their distance. He could barely see to the nearest towers.

He reached the place and cut the throttle. Outside, the lights showed nothing but the rain. He switched them off, pulled up his hood and went out on deck.

Water streamed from every surface, sweeping in sheets across the deck each time the boat rolled in the swell. The boy stood at the gunwale, raised his hands to shield his eyes from the rain and squinted out into the night.

Slowly, his eyes grew more accustomed and he began to make out the pale shapes of the towers looming all around him. He made his way round the deck. There was nothing. The sea slapped quietly against the boat. Of course there was nothing. What had he expected? The rain gusted across his shoulders. If there was nothing there then maybe the boat had gone further, maybe it had … But he stopped the thought before he had finished it. The batteries would have failed. The engine would have given out.

He needed to get back. He turned and crossed the deck. Then he stopped. Out to starboard he could make out the squat shape of a transformer housing. He blinked, wiped the rain from his face. There was something wrong with its silhouette.

He went back into the cabin, switched on the lights and brought the boat round. The headlights swung in an arc through the rain until they hit the transformer, picking out its square angles, its gantry and railings, all highlighted by the streaming water. Then the supports lit up and, as the beams moved through them, there appeared the outlines of a gunwale, the roof of a cabin, the dark mass of a hull.

Tins

The deck rang out as he jumped aboard – a single bass note swallowed up by the rain. He turned on his torch and swung the beam through the sodden air. Dark shapes covered the deck, altering the sounds of the rain as it fell – the patter of bundled tarpaulins and plastic buckets, the rumble of a hollow metal drum.

He hesitated for a moment, moving the torch round slowly. Each dark object the beam picked up made his heart skip over. Finally he forced himself to cross the deck and go into the cabin.

At first it looked the same as the other boat – there was the control panel, the steering column. But, on one side of the cabin, where the built-in lockers should have been, there was a foam roll-matt and a bundle of mouldering sheets.

Moving closer to the control panel, he saw suddenly that it was hollow. A gap on one side of the casing showed that almost all of the wiring and electrics had been pulled out, leaving just the metal shell. The boy crouched down and looked in the hole where the satnav screen should have been. All that was left of the controls were the steering column, battery gauge and the ignition switch. He reached over and pressed it, but nothing happened.

The engine hatch was open and through it he could just make out the engine, or rather the broken and charred remains of the engine. What was left of its workings were scattered around the hull, along with a few tools. The satellite transmitter was on top of the engine housing, scorched and half-melted. The boy shone the torch further in and saw the outline of the battery, then another, and another. There was a whole row of batteries running the length of the keel.

He closed the hatch and stayed squatting in the cabin for a long time. Rain hammered on the roof and the deck. Water ran down from his hair and along his jaw.

He was about to get up when he noticed a sheet of paper tucked into the empty shell of the control panel. He took it out and unfolded it. It was a map of a coastline. The boy looked at it closely, seemed to recognize, for a moment, the shapes of the estuaries and breakwaters, the contours of the seawalls and fences surrounding the warehouses and docks. It was the eastern mainland. He lowered his torch and stood up.

On deck he found a guttering system that had been rigged up to the roof of the cabin and ran down into a large plastic container for collecting rainwater. Towards the stern was a mass of tarpaulin, poles and ropes – the remains of what looked like a shelter for covering the deck. He opened the hold and found it stacked with crates. He climbed down and checked inside them. They were full of tins and supplies – enough to last for months at sea.

It was long into the night before he finally left the boat. If the weather had worsened or the currents had picked up, he could have been in trouble; but the boy was not thinking of that as he piloted back through the dark.

He was thinking about the map and the tins and the row of batteries in the hull. The engine had been modified. There were parts there that weren't in a standard boat. From the quick check the boy had been able to make, it looked like a power converter had been retro-fitted to increase the efficiency. If it had worked it would have more than doubled the output of the batteries. All of the extraneous systems had been stripped out – no lights, no heating, no bilge pump. All of the power had been diverted straight to the engine. With that bank of batteries fully charged, and in the right conditions, it would have had maybe seven or eight times the range of a standard maintenance boat. It could have gone out beyond the borders of the farm. Out of the whole North Sea.

The boy had thought for a long time about the map of the mainland. Why would his father risk going back there? If he had a way out, why not just leave? Then the boy had looked again at the supplies in the hold. There was a spare roll-matt and sheet, two sets of spare clothes, two towels, two mugs and plates and forks – two of everything.

'I'll come back for you,' he'd said. 'Okay?'

But the engine had overheated. The boy had searched the boat, trying to work out what had happened next. Then he'd climbed up to the transformer housing and found the hatch hanging open. Just inside the doorway, a panel had been removed and it looked like an attempt had been made to extract some of the components. Maybe there had been a frayed wire, maybe the water had got in, or maybe it had just been a mistake – a slip of the hand – because all that was left was a gaping hole where the electrics had blown, components thrown about the housing, and the door opposite swinging open into the wind and the sea.

Maybe that was how it had happened, or maybe it had happened differently. The boy had never wanted to imagine his father's last moments. He had always, almost, managed to stop himself before they rose up. And he didn't want to imagine them again now. His whole body felt numb and shaky as he piloted back through the rain – he didn't think he'd ever felt this cold before in his life.

But, either way, however it had happened, his father hadn't given up. He hadn't reneged on anything.

There was a half-empty bottle of homebrew on the table in the galley. The boy sat down and poured himself a drink, drained his mug and poured himself another. Then he got up and closed the galley door, sat back down and shut his eyes.

His thoughts pitched and surged. He tried to order them,

to box them in. He couldn't stop picturing the sheets strewn about the cabin, the twisted tarpaulin and tangles of rope, the engine components scattered around the hull.

He took a deep breath and began to imagine how he'd piece them back together.

Some of them were junk, but others might be serviceable. The row of batteries had looked in good condition. If he could get some charge in them, he could test the electrics and then … He opened his eyes. Then what?

He lifted his mug, caught a nose-full of the foul smell and put it back down on the table. The air con groaned in the walls. The water-filter light flickered and then turned red. The dripping had started up again somewhere. Another crack was working its way across the ceiling.

Then he'd get out. Out of all this. Like his father had planned to do.

His father was good at fixing things – that's what the pilot had said. Well the boy was good at fixing things too. He knew engines, and if could find the right parts then maybe he could get the boat going.

There were footsteps in the corridor and the old man came into the galley. He sat down opposite the boy, placed three lumps of rusted metal on the table, looked down at them and then up at the boy.

The boy ignored the lumps of metal and stared at the old man. His chest tightened. The old man must have known. They were living together on the rig. He must have known what the boy's father had been trying to do.

The old man lifted a finger, then picked up one of the objects, held it next to his ear, shook it very gently and placed it back down on the table to his right. He repeated the process for the other two, placing another on his right and one on his left. Then he leaned back and folded his arms. 'My catch,' he said. 'I have audible and inaudible tins.'

The boy blinked, then looked down at the objects. They were tins – buckled and ballooning with rust, caked in a claggy black substance, but still, it seemed, intact.

Why had the old man stayed? If they'd gone together, if the old man had helped, maybe they'd have been able to fix the engine; maybe they all would have been able to get out.

The old man's hand hovered over the tin on his left, then switched sides and picked up one from his right. He took a penknife from his pocket and scraped round the rim, clearing away the rust and dirt. He blew off the powdery residue, then got up, went to the sink and came back with the tin opener. He sat back down and fitted it to the top of the tin, jolting it around until the wheel bit into the lid.

The boy watched the old man closely. He was turning the handle too fast, so that the wheel kept slipping off the tin; and then he would mutter something, fit it back on and start again. There were streaks of powdery rust on the table and on his hands.

The old man turned the handle again but it didn't move. He tried to take the tin opener off but it was stuck. 'Bloody thing's broken.'

The boy kept watching. All the old man needed to do was turn the wheel backwards but instead he was digging it in even deeper.

The old man pressed harder and the wheel started to bend.

'You're going to break it,' the boy said.

The old man kept turning. Rust flaked off the tin and onto the table.

The boy watched the wheel bend in on itself, like a hot piece of solder. It bent and started to buckle. 'You're going to break it,' the boy said again.

The old man didn't look up. 'It just needs a …'

The boy shook his head. The old man would just carry on. He'd break the tin opener and then they wouldn't be able to open any other food.

The old man gripped the handles tighter. His hands started to shudder.

'You don't care, do you?' the boy said, suddenly.

The old man looked up and frowned.

'Trawling around,' the boy said. 'Digging with poles. Finding junk. You don't care about anything else.'

The old man sat very still. A sharp smell of rust rose up into the room.

'You just carry on,' the boy said. The chill from the rain had started to wear off now. 'You don't care what happens as long as you've got your maps and your nets.'

The old man's hand still gripped the opener, but he didn't make a turn. 'And what,' he said, 'don't I care about?'

The boy shrugged again. 'I don't know. Anything. You'd be happy if we just stayed like this for ever. Eating out of tins, watching the farm fall apart. You wouldn't care if we never got out.'

Still, the old man didn't move. Rust flaked off the tin and onto the table. 'Out,' he said.

'Out of all this. The farm, the Company.'

The old man jerked the opener out of the tin and put it down slowly. 'Who's been talking to you about that?'

'What?'

'Who's been talking to you about that?'

'No one's been talking to me.' The boy looked steadily at the old man. 'No one's been talking to me about anything.'

The old man leaned his elbows on the table and fitted his hands together carefully. The creases over his knuckles deepened. 'There is no out.'

'You don't know that.'

'There is no out.'

'You don't know …'

'No.' The old man stood up quickly. 'You don't know.' He stared down at the tin with his pale eyes, his mouth set, breathing hard, then turned and left the room. 'You don't know anything.'

The boy stayed where he was. He listened to the old man's footsteps, the tap dripping. After a while, he felt his heart rate slow.

He looked down at the tin, then reached over for the old man's penknife, fitted the blade under the half-opened lid and levered it up with a crunch of rust.

A thick and heady scent rose and spread across the room. Sweet, but nothing like coolant or new paint. Sharp, but nothing like salt or metal. It hung in the air, as though it were impossible that it could mix with any other smell on the rig.

The boy could just make out dark lumps floating in a dark liquid. He leaned forward, reached into the tin with the blade of the knife and speared one. When he raised it into the light it shone bright red. The colour was so strange in the monotone room that, for a moment, the boy could not get a clear sense of its outline. It seemed bulbous at one end, tapering down into a rounded point. Yet, despite its strangeness, he could see that it was not a piece of something, not a re-formed shape, but something whole in itself.

He hesitated for a second, then pulled it off the blade. It was soft, but not gelatinous. If he squeezed it, it oozed a syrupy, red liquid and the same heavy scent. When he put it in his mouth, the sweetness was almost unbearable. He bit into it and, for a moment, it was sharp. He chewed and small grains, like fine grit, popped between his teeth. He chewed slowly, until long after he needed to, before swallowing.

Bottles

There was a small collection of spare parts in the cramped store-room off the dock, which the boy had managed to salvage, scrape together and save out over the years.

There was a crate of engine parts, a box of electrical components and a few coils of wire, a single replacement gear wheel and a handful of anemometers. He'd hidden them under a loose floor panel, which could only be accessed by shifting a whole shelving rack out of the way.

He could have used any of these parts a hundred times in the past, but he always tried all other options before he resorted to raiding his dwindling stock.

Right at the bottom of one of the boxes there was a complete socket set, still sealed in brittle, yellowing cellophane. However much he'd wanted to, however difficult the jobs had been, he'd never been able to bring himself to open it. Now, as he sorted through the dusty stock, he picked it up, turned it carefully in his hands, and put it in his toolbag. The cellophane crackled quietly, like a fire. Then he opened the crate containing the engine parts.

The parts were old, but the boy had kept them clean and oiled in case they were ever needed. He used to come in here a lot, to clean and sort things by himself. He liked the smell of oil and dust, and the streaks of old paint on the walls. Whenever the weather had got to him, when there had been endless hail or the air had been daggy for days, he'd come in here. When the farm had pressed in and felt too close, he would sit and imagine all the different uses for the parts – the rows of turbines, the wheels in a gearbox, the patterns on a circuit board … It seemed to help. He shook his head. A good choice, using a tiny cupboard to help him deal with claustrophobia.

He held up a bearing lock and it glinted in the dim light. Well, the parts were needed now. One by one, he removed the components from the boxes and put them in his bag.

From out in the dock he heard the sound of the maintenance boat returning. He quickly moved the rest of the components, shifted the floor panel and shelf back into place and left the storeroom.

The old man was walking across the deck carrying a crate and his poles. As he came down onto the dock, he stopped, put the crate down, bent over and let out a long wheezing breath. The boy stayed where he was. The old man's breath kept coming, like air forcing itself from a pipe, until, just as it seemed there could be no more left in his body, he took a short gasp, gripped the handles of the crate and shut his eyes.

Three long shudders made their way up his back, but he kept his mouth closed and his eyes shut.

The boy walked forwards quietly. The old man stayed where he was, leaning on the crate. As the boy got closer, he could see that it was open and inside there were seven or eight old plastic bottles, cut in half and filled with what looked like mud.

The old man breathed out slowly, reached up and wiped his mouth with the back of his hand. Then he looked up, saw the boy, slammed the lid of the crate shut and carried on up to the rig.

This became their new routine – passing in corridors or on the way down to the boat, exchanging no more than a few words. They were rarely on the rig at the same time, but when they were they would keep to their rooms, avoiding the galley or control room when the other was in there. Some days the boy would be able to take the maintenance boat out first, other days he would have to wait for the old man, then wait for the battery to charge, then finally have a few hours out working on his boat before it got dark.

But the repairs progressed. He managed to drain the water from the keel, reseal the prop shaft and weld up some small leaks in the hull. He cleaned the cabin, tidied up the deck and took stock of the supplies in the hold. One by one, he took the batteries back to the rig, tested and charged them. They all held their charge pretty well. One by one, he took them back to the boat and connected them up.

The engine spares had worked well, but there were still parts that he needed. The drive belt was charred and brittle. A generator belt could be made to work, but they didn't have any in the storeroom. He thought about it for a long time, going through his options. At night, in his room, he read through his technical manuals, looking for any alternatives; but he knew what he needed to do.

He stood in the nacelle and looked down at the generator. He'd removed the casing to reveal the inner workings – the spinning wheels and the drive belt whirring. It was warm in the nacelle, but the boy shivered. Wind pounded on the outer walls. The blades thrummed.

He reached over for the isolator switch. The generator slowed and then stopped.

The nacelle was clean and dry; everything was rust-free and running as it should. He'd spent all day travelling round the farm, searching for a turbine that was in good condition. All day and this was the only one he'd found.

He touched the belt, pressed down to test the flex of the rubber. There were no cracks, no brittleness. It felt almost new. It must have been replaced. Maybe it had been him who had replaced it.

He let go of the belt. Maybe he should find a different one.

A turbine that was about to give out, but that still, for some reason, had a new drive belt? He shook his head. No, it had to be this one.

He hadn't checked the maintenance reports in weeks; but every time he happened to glance at the system he saw that the numbers had dropped. They'd soon be below fifty per cent. What difference would one turbine make?

He took a pry bar out of his toolbag and began to work the belt off the wheels.

The old man was waiting in the dock when the boy brought the boat back in. The boy threw over the mooring rope, but the old man just stood there, staring out of the dock gates. The boy climbed out of the boat and moored it up himself.

'You manage to fix it then?'

The boy looked up at the old man. 'What?'

'Did you manage to fix it?' The old man looked at the boy. 'The transformer you've been going back to.'

'Oh …' The boy picked up the charging cable and took it over to the socket. 'Yeah.'

'What was wrong?'

'What?'

The old man was still looking at the boy. 'What was wrong?'

'The fan.'

'Must've been a big job.'

'Yeah, I suppose.'

'You've been going back enough.'

'It was a big job.'

The old man nodded and turned back to the gates. 'How'd you fix it?'

'What?'

'How did you fix it?'

'I fitted a new motor.'

'Had a spare one with you?'

'Yeah.'

'I didn't know we had a spare one.'

'We did.' The boy got his stuff and made to leave the dock.

The old man nodded. 'I didn't see it on the maintenance report.'

The boy stopped. The old man never looked at the reports. He crouched down, unzipped his toolbag, zipped it back up again.

The old man walked over to the charging point. 'So is this battery almost done, or what?'

'I've only just plugged it in.'

'What's it on?'

'Thirty per cent.'

'That'll do.' The old man unplugged the cable, climbed over the gunwale onto the boat.

The boy stayed on the dock. 'That'll do for what?'

The old man went into the cabin and switched on the engine. 'I thought we'd go and do some work.'

'What?'

'Some work.' The old man came back to the cabin door. 'You know, like you've just been doing.'

'It's getting dark.'

'We've got lights.'

'The battery's low.'

'It'll do.' The old man climbed back out of the boat and made his way towards the boy's toolbag. 'We can go back over where you just were, see if we can fix some more of those turbines. Get them yùnzhuǎn.'

The boy stepped forward and blocked his path. 'Why do you want to do it now?'

The old man shrugged. 'I feel like it.'

'But why now?'

The old man was so close that the boy could see the dark fleck in the corner of his left eye. He'd got it one winter, when a flywheel they'd been working on had suddenly shattered in the cold, throwing out splinters of metal. The boy had got three in his forearm and one in his neck. He'd pulled his out straight away but the old man had left his eye alone, saying that the metal would work its way out eventually, or work its way further in and disappear and then he could forget about it. But in the end it had just stayed where it was, floating.

The old man frowned. 'Why don't you want me to go?'

The boy took a step back. 'I don't not want …'

'You bloody moan at me day after week, year after month. And now, I say let's go and do some work and you don't want to.' The old man walked past the boy and picked up the toolbag. Then he untied the moorings and pushed the boat off from the dock.

'All right, hang on, I'll …'

'I'm not bloody hanging on.' The old man turned and pointed a finger at the boy. 'I'm going to go on my own. You're bloody disinvited.'

The boy watched as the boat pulled out of the dock, then he ran up to the control room and switched on the map. The maintenance boat's symbol was heading south, straight towards the transformer where the other boat was moored. The boy watched the screen, watched the symbol creep further on.

Then it stopped. The boy held his breath and watched, but the boat didn't move. He breathed out slowly, checked the coordinates and brought up the footage from the nearest working camera. The screen was turning an inky blue, but he could just make out the boat, moored up to a stopped turbine, and the dark smudge of a figure climbing the ladder up to the jacket, carrying a large bag.

The boy watched the screen. After almost an hour, just as the last light was beginning to fail, he saw the blades of the turbine begin to turn.

The first thing the boy did the next time he went out was move the boat. He started moving it every few days, towing it to different areas of the farm, mooring it up to different turbines and transformers, then taking long detours on his way back to the rig. He couldn't risk the old man noticing something again.

The new belt fitted perfectly and the engine was almost finished. The only problem was the power converter. The extra input had been too much for it and had caused the whole thing to overheat. Even if he took the one from the maintenance boat, it would just do the same again.

The boy sat in the hull, staring at the engine and thinking. He thought of all of the components in all of the turbines and transformers across the farm. There was nothing he could use. He thought of all the machinery in the rig; he went through it, level by level, corridor by corridor – the dock controls, the water system, the air con, the galley, his room, the old man's. He stopped. The boat rocked and a screwdriver at his feet rolled from side to side. There was one way he could get what he needed.

Anything you want – that's what the pilot had said.

He listened to the old man moving about the rig. He listened to him in the galley, packing his bag, taking food and drink – he would be gone all day. He listened to the old man walking down the stairs and into the dock. And he listened long after he had heard the boat's engine recede into the distance.

He got up off his bed and went out of his room. He hadn't slept, but he didn't feel tired. He knew what he needed to get – what wouldn't be missed – and he knew where he would hide it until the next resupply.

He walked down the corridor in his socks, the fabric sticking to the floor. At the door to the old man's room he paused, went over, once more, the same thoughts that had been circling in his head all night: he was doing it for both of them. If he could get the boat working then they could both get out. If, in the end, the old man didn't want to go, then that was his choice. But the boy had to try.

100

He turned the handle and pushed the door slowly, but it didn't touch against anything. He waited for a moment, then opened it fully and stood in the doorway. There was the old man's room – his bed, his chair, his clothes, his crates; but in place of the piles of trawled-up bones and pebbles and pieces of wood, there were hundreds of plastic bottles with their tops cut off, full of sand and silt and mud.

c.20,000 Before Present

This is how the landscape forms: by increments, by the steady acquisition of layers.

First, the ice pulls back like curling fingers, leaving bare rock and frozen ground – the world stripped back to its bones.

Then pale flecks appear: pollen grains blown north. They land and settle, gathering in the cracks like snow. They wait for enough warmth to split open, enough moisture to put down roots. They gather in the cracks, waiting for the real snow to thaw.

Minerals crystallize.

Lichens grow, like rock from rock, less than a millimetre a year.

*

Moss follows.

Then a thread of wild flowers. They have been waiting in crevices, following seams of thawing soil. They bloom in a sudden shot of colour, thin and fragile as a vein.

But enough to draw in beetles and minute flies, which settle, breed and expire, leaving a layer of wings and chitin.

Birds and small mammals come next. They leave footprints and bones pressed into the mud. They carry seeds that have tangled in their feathers and fur.

The seeds fall to the ground and grow, sending up shoots to meet the wind, which twists and bends them, pummelling them horizontal.

All things proceed laterally.

Whole trees grow, spreading their branches no more than a few inches from the ground.

A forest grows inch-deep on the rocks.

The first herds of reindeer come and graze down any shoots that break the snow-line.

*

And following the reindeer, like ghosts, are their own hooves and antlers and skin, cut and sewn to fit the shapes of other bodies, which spread north, leaving their own traces in turn.

Footprints, handprints, the remnants of fires.

They are deep inland, but their pockets are lined with dentalium shells. As they walk, they roll cowries between their fingers.

Knots

When had the old man done it? When had he taken all of his stuff off the rig? And where the hell had he put it all?

The boy tried to think back to the times he'd watched the old man going out on the boat. When had he taken crates with him? Where had he gone with them? The boy hadn't been paying attention. He'd been so focused on fixing the boat that he hadn't noticed anything the old man was doing.

He considered offering the pilot turbine parts, but that wouldn't work. The pilot had demanded almost a whole nacelle just for a box of poles. The boy needed to get him something he wanted. There was no other option.

He began watching the old man constantly, tracking his movements on the satellite map, noting down the coordinates of every turbine or transformer he stopped at. Then, when the old man came back to the rig, the boy would take the boat out and retrace his winding path, visiting and checking each location in turn. But he never seemed to be able to follow the old man's route exactly. He would plot the coordinates on the satnav, but always find himself off-course. The screen would show that he was heading towards a transformer, but the transformer would never appear. He spent hours trying to find a turbine that he'd seen the old man go inside on five different occasions. When he finally reached it, after travelling up and down the same row three times, he found the outer hatch completely rusted shut.

Then there was the problem of the battery. However he ran the engine, whichever route he took around the towers, he never seemed to be able to get the charge to last as long as the old man had. Even when he followed the satnav precisely, even when he chose the most direct routes, he found himself fighting against rip currents, or getting lost among the identical rows.

There were turbines that the old man visited that the boy had never even been able to get to. Every time he tried he was forced to turn back, the battery dropping to fifty per cent before he'd even got close. The old man would go to these turbines regularly, spending all day out there before taking a circuitous route back. Sometimes, after the old man returned, the boy would go down to the dock to check the battery and find it still on twenty or thirty per cent.

He thought about giving up on trying to follow the old man and instead just search the farm systematically, working through it turbine by turbine, row by row. But there were so many turbines, there were so many rows. And what would stop the old man deciding, at any time, to move his stuff to one of the turbines that the boy had already checked? He could end up searching the farm for ever.

Sometimes, if he came across one of the old man's nets, he would haul it up and sort through its contents, to see if he could find anything that resembled the objects that used to be in the old man's room. Sometimes he found things that looked like pins, or beads, or small figures; but when he brought them back to his room and cleaned them, they just melted into grit and sludgy clay.

There was a turbine up in the north of zone two – the only one working in a broken row.

The boy had seen the old man go back to it several times. He only ever stayed there for a few minutes. Not long enough to make repairs, or set up a net, or assemble and disassemble his poles. But maybe long enough to go and check on something that he'd hidden.

The old man had taken the boat out the day before and not got back until late, so the boy would be able to argue the use of it that morning, if it came to it. He went into the control room to check the turbine's coordinates one last time. But then, as he was about to leave, he noticed the weather report. There was a warning of a storm front pushing in from the north-west. It would hit the farm by the middle of the day. The boy sat down and looked at the map. He centred it on the turbine in zone two. The other screens showed the angles from the nearest cameras. It was too far away. He'd never make it there and back in time.

'You wanting the boat?' the old man said from the corridor.

The boy quickly switched the screen back to the weather report. 'There's a storm coming in,' he said.

'So, no, then.' The old man came into the room.

The boy turned round to look at him, then froze. The old man was wearing the fur hat. He'd pulled it down low at one side, so that it looked almost jaunty. The dark fur gleamed under the strip lights.

The old man looked over the boy's shoulder at the screens. He looked at the weather report, then each of the camera angles. He frowned, glanced at them one more time, then turned and walked away down the corridor.

The boy stayed where he was. His hand went up and rubbed slowly along his jaw. Where had he left the hat? He couldn't remember where he'd put it after the pilot had given it to him – in the galley with the resupply? Or had he left it in his room? Either way, the old man had found it and now he knew … now he knew what? There was nothing for him to know. It was a hat. That was it.

He turned back to the screens and saw the storm warning again. It had gone up another level – the storm would be big and it was spreading fast.

The boy got up and ran after the old man. 'Did you hear what I said?'

The old man carried on walking. 'There's a storm coming in.'

'So where are you going?'

The old man picked up a bag that he'd left outside his room. 'Out.'

'But …'

The old man turned. 'Why are you so interested in where I'm going?'

The boy stopped. 'I'm not.'

The old man stared at him. 'You been making many repairs recently?'

The boy looked down at the floor. 'Some.'

'You've been out a lot.'

'So have you.'

The old man adjusted the hat carefully. 'I was up a turbine the other day and I saw the generator belt was missing.'

The boy kept his eyes fixed on the floor. 'It must have broken.'

'Not broken. There were no bits anywhere. Just missing.'

The boy looked up and held the old man's gaze. 'What do you want me to do about it?'

The old man stared at the boy for a long time. Then he sighed quietly. 'What did he say to you?'

'Who?'

'The fat man. At the last resupply. What did he say to you?'

The boy took a breath. There was some loose stitching on one of the flaps of the hat. It needed fixing or it would make a hole. 'Nothing.'

'He doesn't know what he's talking about. He's trying to get to you.'

A light on the air-con dial on the wall flashed slowly. The boy watched it and thought about the prop shaft he'd managed to reconnect on the boat. It turned so smoothly now. He almost wanted to tell the old man about it; and about the intricate way that the batteries connected up; and how, when he was working on the boat, he could almost hear his father just behind him, his footsteps, the sound of him bending down to fit a part; how he could almost see him over his shoulder, smell the dusty smokiness on his breath. The light flashed again. 'He didn't say anything.'

The old man took a step forward, then stopped. 'Jem,' he said.

The boy didn't move.

The old man lifted his bag onto his shoulder. He suddenly looked tired. 'I'll see you later.' He turned and walked down the corridor towards the dock, the hat pulled down low over his eyes.

The boy let out a long breath and was about to go back to the control room, when he remembered. 'What about the storm?' he called down the corridor, but he could already hear the clang of the dock gates.

He watched through the rig's cameras as the old man piloted the boat out of the dock, then he switched to the satellite map. The weather report showed that the storm was only an hour away. The swell was already picking up, thumping higher against the rig's supports. The old man was heading north, straight towards the turbine that the boy had just been looking at, straight towards the storm.

The boat travelled further from the rig. The weather report showed the front pushing closer to the farm. It cycled down from the northern ocean, spreading outwards like something dark that had spilled. The wind speed increased and clouds ballooned up through the atmosphere. Eventually the boat came to a stop at the turbine. The boy waited, watching the report. The storm came closer. The old man was still moored up to the turbine, just a few miles from where it would hit. The boy took out his watch. He switched from the weather report to the satellite map and back again. The boat symbol didn't move. He searched for any available cameras, but the signal was scrambled by the weather. It was exactly midday when the computer showed the storm sweeping through the north fields of the farm.

The boy got up and went outside to the gangway, which ran around the upper levels of the rig.

The swell was washing over the jackets of the towers. Spray swept across in waves, soaking the boy's face. In the distance, to the north, the turbines were feathering their blades. And further beyond that, a thick murky line grew on the horizon. It was brown but glowing, almost bronze. The boy stood, holding on to the rail, and watched as the swell rose, the wind increased and then … nothing.

The clouds didn't come any closer. They edged along the horizon and then vanished from sight. Soon after, the waves dropped and the wind returned to its normal level. All around, the turbines engaged their yaw motors and angled back into the wind. The boy let go of the rail. His fingers were locked stiff and his knuckles were raw. He clenched and unclenched his hands as he made his way slowly back into the rig.

The weather report had changed to show the storm front veering east well before it reached the farm. The boy switched off the screen and sat down. Then he turned the screen back on and brought up the satellite map. It was still zoomed in on the turbine, but the maintenance boat wasn't there. He rescaled the map until he found the boat. It was on a course back to the rig, travelling at an angle from a different part of the farm.

The next day the boy went out and searched the turbine. But all he found was the fur hat, on the floor in the middle of the empty tower.

The old man's routes changed. He started visiting the same locations over and over. One day the boy saw him go back to the same three turbines he'd visited just days before. The boy had been out to them and found nothing. Indeed, it didn't seem that the old man was going to them for any reason at all. He didn't set his nets or assemble his poles. He just went in, then came back out and stood in the doorway looking out at the sea.

It was only when the old man finally made his way back to the rig that the boy realized what was happening. The old man was following the exact route that the boy had taken when he came back from checking the turbines, even down to the detour where he'd strayed off-course.

The boy sat back in his chair and stared at the screen. Now the old man was following him.

After that, the boy had to be careful. He began moving randomly about the farm, taking long detours and avoiding the cameras. He made sure he took his toolbag up into every tower he visited and then sat in the nacelle until he thought the old man would have got bored watching. While he was there, he always made some kind of repair, even if nothing needed doing – removing all the wheels from the gearbox and then fitting them back on, leaving the case open, so it would be obvious if the old man came to check.

He only went to his boat when it was dark or foggy, and he always covered his tracks – travelling in sweeping arcs around the farm, making himself visible at other turbines to throw the old man off.

In the meantime, he watched the old man carefully, making a note of any new or different journey that he took.

And the old man watched the boy. They shadowed each other's movements, visiting the same turbines over and over, waiting for the other to crack or slip up as they traced ever more complex and circuitous routes through the farm.

The boy lay on his bed, watching the air con shift dust particles in loops and spirals around the room. He breathed slowly, curled and uncurled his toes, watched the dust. It was surprising, really, how much of it there was. The air con had filters and the door was always closed, so all the dust in the room must have come from him. This was his body in particle form, breaking apart, cell by cell, to fill the space.

The old man had just come back and was unloading the boat. It would be some time before the battery was charged enough, so there was nothing to do but wait. The boy rolled onto his side and picked up one of the technical manuals from under his bedside unit.

He looked down at the columns of text, the graphs and tables of figures. There were solutions here for almost every fault or malfunction that could occur on the farm. But he couldn't focus on it – there was no point focusing on it. The dust moved slowly around the room. He put the book back on the floor.

There were steps in the hallway and three short, sharp coughs, then the door swung open. The old man strode into the middle of the room holding a length of rope.

The boy put his hands behind his head and looked up at the ceiling.

The old man held up the rope. 'Do you know what this is?'

The boy kept his eyes on the ceiling. If he didn't answer then maybe the old man would go away. He waited a full minute. 'It's a bit of rope,' he said finally.

'Not *that*. This.'

The boy looked at the old man. He was still holding up the rope. The boy looked at it, then back at the old man.

'I don't use this knot,' the old man said.

The boy closed his eyes.

'I don't use this knot,' the old man said again. 'One of my nets had moved and it was tied up with this and I don't ever use this knot.'

The boy opened his eyes and looked at the knot. 'Why not?'

The old man's grip tightened on the rope. 'What?'

'Why don't you use it?' It looked like a round turn and two half hitches. It was a good, strong knot.

The old man narrowed his eyes. 'Because I use a rolling hitch.'

'That's better than a rolling hitch.'

'That's not better than a bloody rolling hitch.' He threw the rope onto the bed and began pacing the room.

The boy sat up and picked up the rope. 'How'd you get it off?'

The old man stopped pacing. 'What?'

'It's still got the loop in it. How'd you get it off?'

'I untied it, didn't I.'

'So who tied this one?'

'I did.'

'I thought you said you couldn't tie it.'

'Couldn't tie it?' The old man took a step towards the boy.

'I thought you said …'

'I can tie more bloody knots than you!'

The boy looked at the old man. 'So you do use it.'

'I never use it.'

'But you just did.'

'Only to show you that I don't.'

The boy looked down at the rope, turned it over slowly. 'So you're saying, whoever tied this knot moved your net?'

'Exactly.'

The boy threw the rope back to the old man. 'You tied this knot.'

The old man stood still. His jaw twitched. He gripped the rope in his fist, held it up in front of him, then turned and left the room, letting the heavy door thud shut behind him.

The boy stayed on the bed for a moment. Then he got up, took a cloth from the bucket under the sink and wiped away the damp, brown footprints the old man had left.

He lay back down. Now, the dust in the room was the old man's too – all tangled up with his own. If he thought about it, he could imagine them both swirling around, caught by the air con's mechanical breeze, dragged through its vents and grilles, through all the rig's pipework and out into the air. He could almost feel the real wind carrying them up over the fields, over the cushion of turbulence and out to the open water, the featureless sea, where all noise and trace of the farm diminished.

But he tried not to think about it too much. All the dust got caught in the filters.

Circuits

With each concussion, the balls jolted and shook. They had to count the wave periods and time their shots, the weather dictating their pace of play, until the rhythms became so practised that it seemed as if each strike of the cue, each glance off the cushion, were predicting the pattern of the storm.

The pool table was missing four balls, including the white, and had two buckled legs that needed propping up to even the surface. The remaining balls were chipped and riddled with hairline cracks; some were dented, so that they swung when struck or else skidded along the ripped baize. As such, balls and pockets were assigned different values, and points were scored for potting certain balls in certain pockets or keeping balls out of areas marked by scratches, tears and abrasions. If balls were potted in either of the pockets that had lost their runners, they fell to the floor and had to be given to the opposing player. One of the cues was snapped to half the length of the other, so whoever used it received a handicap, which varied each time they played, as did their memory and implementation of the rules.

They circled the table, keeping to opposite sides. This was the first rule of play. The second was that no one was allowed to talk. They had been playing frame after frame, day after day, night after night. They couldn't leave the rig. They had exhausted all other jobs and possible pastimes. They had tried to keep to themselves, but had reached the limit of what boredom they could endure. So they had gravitated to the rec room, picked up their cues and started the game, just as they always did when they were stuck in the worst and longest of storms.

They circled the table and the boy tried not to look out of the window at the waves that rose up into the sky, as if they were being acted upon by some enormous, sweeping magnet. He tried not to listen as they boomed through the rig's supports. He tried not to think of his boat out there, moored to its turbine, miles away in the fields.

He circled the table, crouched down and lined up his next shot.

There had been no warning of the storm, no sign of any kind. The weather report had predicted nothing but clear skies, maybe a slight increase in wind speed. Then the boy had looked up and seen a shadowy patch on one of the screens. He'd leaned forward, tried to wipe it off, then noticed that it had appeared on the other screens as well. He had switched to the cameras in the northern fields just in time to see the sky turn completely dark and, one by one, the turbines feather their blades.

He'd watched as the storm swept through the farm. He'd watched the cameras blur then white out, the output drop. He'd watched the sky turn yellow, then green, then murky red. He'd listened to the pitch of the wind, felt the growing weight of the waves slam into the rig's supports. Then he'd gone to the window and watched the whole world turn to water.

Waves rose up like buildings, breaking against the towers and shooting spray up to meet the rain, which twisted and swept at angles and drove back down to the sea. The water swelled above the jackets of the turbines, up to the tips of the blades, which hung still while everything lurched around them. All except for a row of seven turbines, out in the distance, which still beat frantically, their wind sensors or their blade motors malfunctioning.

The boy had stood at the window for a long time, unable to look away. Only then, suddenly, had he thought of his boat.

He'd run down to the dock, heard the cacophony of the ringing walls, seen the usually still water inside start to prickle with waves, and known then that there was nothing he could do. He couldn't go out. He couldn't go anywhere. He'd turned back to the stairs, then noticed the deck of the maintenance boat piled up with the old man's nets. He must have gone out early that morning and gathered them in before the boy was even awake.

* * *

119

The cameras greyed out or were torn from their housings. The connection to the central system went down. There were no weather reports. The satellite map scrambled. The world shrank to the metres between bed and washroom, washroom and galley, galley and pool table.

They would circle the table all day and all night. They would play on to the point of exhaustion. Yet they would still be too restless to sleep. The rig seemed to draw in the energy of the storm, storing it in its metal shell. When the boy walked down the narrow corridors, his skin would tingle and his hands twitch. If he brushed his arm against a wall or doorframe, the hairs would rise.

The automatic lights shorted out, as did the morning alarm. The boy tried to reset them, but the timer must have gone, because the lights started dimming in the middle of the day and the alarm went off just as it was getting dark.

Outside, the days became almost as dark as the nights. They played on regardless. In between shots, the boy would look out of the window trying to judge, by the quality of greyness, whether it was morning or evening, noon or dusk, but any change in light or colour bore no relation to the time of day.

Sometimes the sky was a depthless black, but the sea somehow shone silver and yellow. Sometimes the sea would be dark and the sky would be almost white with spray. Then a sudden sheet of lightning would throw itself to every horizon, illuminating the storm in its enormity and flooding the room with a light so clear it caused even the strip lights to cast clean-edged shadows.

One day, or maybe night, he glanced out of the window and saw a light – a single light, flickering out in the dark. Then another appeared, and another, until there were seven, strung out in a row. He stood, staring, until he finally realized what they were – the turbines that had failed to feather their blades had finally overheated and burst into flames. The lights stayed for minutes, or maybe hours, before, one by one, they were extinguished by the rain.

As they played, they added more rules – that a ball could only be potted if it had first come off a cushion, that a ball could only be played against a cushion if it had first come off another ball – dragging the games out, making them more complex, until there was no end in sight.

Whatever the rules, they both played the same way they always played – the old man working the angles, the boy favouring the long shot, both of them knowing exactly what the other would do next.

Sometimes, one of them would lose concentration, or the other, in a moment of inspiration, would pot three balls in a row. Then the game would suddenly change. The one in the lead would play quickly and try to pressure the other into rushing his shots. The one losing would become careful, defensive; digging in; forcing the play back to stasis.

* * *

Finally, the old man slept. He finished a bottle of homebrew and slumped over the table, still standing, his face resting on the baize. His hand twitched against his cue. The boy found a blanket and covered him. When the old man woke up, the blanket fell onto the floor and they started playing again.

Water forced its way in through pipes and ducts, through the hatches, through the rivets in the walls and the sealant round the window. Water trickled from vents, ran down gantries.

The boy put out tins to catch the drips. When the tins filled, he went round emptying them into a crate, which he took down and emptied into the dock – returning water to water.

This became the only way to tell how many days had passed. The inches of water collected in the tins, the number of crates emptied into the dock.

One night, the old man was about to take his shot when a deep grinding sound reverberated through the walls. He and the boy stepped back from the table and steadied themselves. The rig shook, seemed to sway, and then all of the balls slowly slumped against one cushion.

The boy stood upright, tilted his head one way then the other. He went to the table, picked up a ball and put it on the floor. It stayed there for a moment, then rolled slowly across the room and bumped into the old man's boot. The old man looked down at the ball, then up at the boy. They both stood still and waited, feeling for any movement with each successive thump of the waves.

They stayed there until the window paled to galvanized steel, but there was no further slippage.

After a few days they'd stopped noticing the tilt. The only difference was that the floor's new angle served to correct the listing of the pool table, so they no longer needed to prop up the buckled legs.

Systems

The boy woke to the strangest sound – a sort of hissing, like air escaping from a broken compressor. He lay in bed listening for a long time before he realized that it was his own breath – a sound he hadn't heard since the storm began. He moved his hands and heard his fingers rasp against the sheets. Then, gradually, he made out the air con, the water system and, from two floors up, the computer rebooting. He jumped out of bed, gathered together his tools and a tow rope and made for the dock.

The maintenance boat was ready to go. He'd kept it charged all through the storm, so at the first opportunity he could go out and check on his boat. He ran down the stairs, his boots echoing off the metal. But when he got down there, the engine was already switched on, the dock gates open and the old man was standing at the wheel.

The boy stopped in the doorway. 'You going out?' he said.

'Thought I might.'

The boy cursed himself for not waking earlier.

'I thought we could take a little trip,' the old man said.

'A trip where?'

'I thought you could tell me.'

The boy felt his mouth go dry. 'There'll be lots of work to do. I think zone two caught the worst of it.'

The old man looked down at the tow rope. 'Work? Is that what you were planning on doing?'

The boy looked down at the tow rope. The old man would find out anyway. When the boy brought the boat back to the rig he'd see for himself. That's if there was anything left of the boat to bring back. The boy climbed on board, threw the rope in the corner of the cabin and walked over to the wheel.

The old man stared at the boy and didn't move out of the way.

The boy stopped. 'If you want me to take you there, I'm driving.'

The old man stayed staring at the boy for a moment, then stepped back from the wheel.

They travelled out in silence. The sea was calm, the sky a milky white. The only signs of the storm were a few less turning blades and a few more towers leaning at precarious new angles. One tower had a gash down its flank; another had a dent half the size of the maintenance boat pressed into the metal.

'Why didn't you tell me?' the boy said.

The old man said nothing.

'I found his boat.' The boy looked in the mirror and saw the old man turn away to the window.

'Why didn't you tell me he was trying to get out?'

Still the old man said nothing.

The boy cut the engine and turned away from the wheel. 'Why didn't you tell me anything?'

The old man carried on looking out of the window. 'What good would it have done?' he said quietly.

'I'd have known.' The boy took a step forward. 'He didn't just give up.'

'He did give up.'

'He was good at fixing things. He had a plan. I'd have …'

'You'd have what?' The old man turned from the window and took a step towards the boy. 'You'd have done exactly what he did. Got some idiotic notion in your head. Obsessed over it for years instead of keeping your head down. And then, when it didn't work out …' He stopped, looked past the boy out of the window and frowned.

The boy followed where the old man was looking. There was just the farm – the sea and sky as calm as they had been before. He was about to speak, but the old man had already moved past him and taken hold of the wheel. He hit the accelerator and turned the boat in a tight circle.

The boy stumbled and banged against the side window. 'What the hell are you doing?'

'Storm's coming back.'

'There's no storm.'

'Fast.' The old man increased the power and the boat thumped over the water.

'Wait.' The boy staggered to the front of the cabin. 'We've got to go back for the boat. It might still be there.'

The old man didn't answer. He was staring ahead and kept glancing in the mirror.

The boy reached over and cut the power.

'What are you doing?' the old man shouted.

The boy put his hand on the wheel. 'I can get it to work. I know how. We can both get out.'

The old man put both hands on the wheel and tried to shove the boy away. 'We don't have time for this.'

The boy gripped harder and stayed where he was. Heat rose up his chest, his neck, lodged in the backs of his eyes. The old man had his head buried in the mud and silt and clay of the seabed. He would keep them both stuck out there for ever.

The old man shoved again. He looked up at the boy and the boy looked down at him and they stood in silence, wrestling with the wheel, while the boat bobbed among the towers and, far out to the west, the waves began to rise.

The old man's arms were starting to shake, the veins standing out on the backs of his hands. The boy inched the wheel his way and gritted his teeth. 'He was going to come and get me out.' He inched the wheel again. 'He had a plan. He was going to come to the mainland and then get us both out.' He planted his foot forward and shoved his way between the old man and the wheel. 'And you didn't say anything. You just let me think that he—'

Suddenly the old man let go and swung his fist, catching the boy on the ear.

The boy stepped back. He raised his hand to his ear.

'Well he did, didn't he?' The old man stood with his hands on his knees, breathing heavily. 'If you've seen that boat, you'll know it could never have worked. He knew it too and he took off in it anyway. He knew exactly what he was doing.' The old man wiped his mouth and turned back to the wheel. 'And he knew what'd happen when he didn't come back. That you'd end up out here. That you'd have to take his place. I told him. You think he was thinking about you when he did it? You're as bloody stupid as he was.'

The boy stood still. His ear stung. He stretched his jaw. Then he grabbed the old man and wrenched him away from the controls. As he did it, the old man pulled on the throttle and the boat lurched sharply. The boy stumbled and fell, his elbow driving into the old man's chest. The old man hit the ground and doubled over. For a moment he was silent, unmoving, his body curled, then he let out a long, gasping breath. His chest shuddered and his legs twitched. And then he began to cough.

The boy pushed himself up, tried to steady himself against the tilting deck and the movement of the boat, which was turning in a tight circle. The sky wheeled around the cabin.

He staggered to the controls and cut the throttle. The boat slowed, stilled and righted itself, rising and falling in the swell.

He crouched down by the old man, reached out, but stopped just short of touching him. 'I …' He breathed heavily, swallowed.

He stood up and went over to the control panel, switched on the satnav and entered the coordinates for the tower where he had last moored his boat. The screen flickered. He hit the side of the control panel and the picture stabilized. He turned the wheel and pushed down hard on the throttle.

The waves were growing. Behind him there was a smudge of black on the horizon. Just a few feet away, against the wall of the cabin, the old man lay, eyes screwed tight shut, still coughing and shaking. But the boy tried not to think of that. He just watched the flickering satnav screen, squinted out of the windows, scoured the rows. He knew he should be close, but the screen kept glitching, the symbols jumping from place to place.

Then he saw it – two rows ahead, swinging loose from the foot of a tower. One of the mooring lines had snapped and the boat was wallowing low in the water, but it was still there.

It took time to pilot in against the swell, but eventually he managed to come in close to the lee of the tower. He ran out on deck, tied the tow-line to the stern and then reached out with a boathook, pulled the other boat alongside and climbed aboard. He released the mooring cable and the two boats drifted free from the tower. Then he secured the tow-line to the bow, jumped back over to the maintenance boat, went into the cabin and stood for a moment to catch his breath.

It was only then that he noticed how dark it had become.

Clouds banked up in a vast semicircle, spreading out from the west. All the turbines had turned, and were facing into the clouds, beating hard.

The rig was over there, somewhere towards the swelling storm. The satnav screen fuzzed and pixelated. The old man was still lying on the floor. The only sounds were the wind, the engine and the old man's coughing. And then there was a flash and a shuddering rumble, as though something too tightly wound had snapped.

The boy took a step towards the window, then a step back to the control panel. He checked the battery gauge, then the satnav. He turned the satnav off. He looked down at the old man, then out of the window. He stood in the middle of the cabin, closed his eyes and tried to order his thoughts.

Here were the things he knew:

They were over an hour from the rig, and only then if he could run at full speed; but towing the other boat would slow them down.

The storm was moving fast, advancing across the sky, swallowing field after field.

It would get to the rig before them.

If they tried to get back to the rig it would catch them in the middle of the fields.

The storm was going to catch them, that was a certainty.

The only choice he had was where that happened.

He opened his eyes. So then, there was only one option.

A heavy swell came in and caught them broadside, but he used it to swing the boat round, giving it enough power at the last moment to keep them steady and move them into the middle of the channel between the towers. The key was to conserve the battery, to use the current where he could, let the front push them east, towards the open water between the zones.

He thought about how the old man would pilot the boat, how he would handle the wheel, use the waves that spread from the bases of the towers to carry them along. He tried not to think of him lying on the floor at the side of the cabin, coughing and convulsing with each breath.

The storm was gaining on them; the swell increased; all around, the turbines slowed and feathered their blades as the wind passed beyond the upper threshold. Then, suddenly, the towers thinned to open water. The boy let the swell carry them further. Now they were out of the fields, he left the wheel, made sure the windows were secure and bolted the cabin door. The old man had stopped coughing, but was still lying on the floor, shaking and breathing heavily. The boy went to the locker, took a strap off one of the toolbags, tied it to a handle on the cabin wall and hooked it over one of the old man's arms. The old man's eyes were closed, but he gripped hold of the strap. The boy went back to the wheel and turned the boat to face the waves. The last turbines of the field were swallowed up by cloud.

He wondered how big the storm was. He could no longer see the edges of the front. It had spread so that it filled the entire hemisphere of the sky. He wondered how long it would last. Hours? Days? It didn't really matter. The battery was on sixty per cent; once it ran dry, events would take care of themselves. He took his watch out of his pocket and checked the time. It was only then that he noticed his hands were shaking.

The old man had opened his eyes and was sitting up against the cabin wall, holding on to the strap. The boy thought he saw him nod, but it was hard to be sure in the movement of the boat.

He wondered if this was the same storm that had hit them before. How would he know? Could he call it the same storm if it was composed of entirely new molecules of water and air? He had read, in one of the technical manuals, that all fluid systems were fundamentally similar, sharing an ordered pattern of chaos and complexity. He had thought about that for a long time. How randomness could form a pattern, which would never really be a pattern because it would always be different. So even if there were two storms made of exactly the same molecules, in exactly the same proportions, hitting in exactly the same place, they still wouldn't be exactly the same storm.

He was almost glad when the first wave broke against the bow, because then he thought of nothing at all.

The boat rose and fell, like a piston powered by the waves. The storm pushed and tore in all directions. The boy increased the power, driving the boat to stillness. The only sign that time had passed was the gradual fall of the battery meter. And, at some point, the dark of the storm was joined by the dark of night.

Everything shrank to the hazy limit of the boat's lights – a bubble of bright turbulence, encompassing the vessel. Water squeezed in from under the sealant. Water flushed across the deck. A fist of water beat on the window and, when it cleared, left a delicate web of fracture lines in the glass. There was a faint smell of smoke, then the wipers slowed and stopped. The oncoming waves were reduced to glimpses between the sheets of water that swept down the windscreen.

The boy clung to the wheel, tried to keep his footing. The locker burst open and its contents flew across the cabin. The old man sat braced in the corner, hanging on grimly, staring straight ahead. There was a crash from the deck and, through the rear window, the boy saw that the cleat he had tied the tow-line to had been wrenched loose and was close to breaking off.

He locked the wheel, unbolted the door and was knocked off his feet as the wind threw it open. He thought he heard the old man's voice, but it was drowned out by the clamour. He crawled back towards the doorway and out onto the deck, grabbing on to anything he could to stop himself sliding. A wave dumped down and flushed through his overalls from neck to ankles. He reached the tow-line and caught hold of the loose end. He turned to try to find somewhere more secure to tie it and another load of spray hit him square in the face. He stood, coughing, wiping his eyes, holding the tow-line in one hand. There was a judder as the cleat finally broke free. The rope slackened for a moment, the boy opened his eyes, and only just saw the slope of the wave – a gleaming wall in the glow of the lights – before it slid beneath the boat, tilting him backwards, lifting his feet from the deck.

c.14,000 Before Present

The sea has never been so far away.

At some point the wind eased enough for stems to straighten. At some point the earth warmed enough for roots to work their way down and anchor the swaying mass of trees.

The landscape grows in three dimensions – taproot to trunk, trunk to thicket, thicket to woodland to forest. Things are stable, things hold their ground. Nothing is undermined. Nothing slips.

But this is all still water's work.

This is water turning to solid mass, taking its liquid forms – ripple, eddy, vortex – and translating them to tendril, flower, leaf. This is water reaching skywards, arching and holding its shape.

*

This is water repeating itself. Cells dividing like foam, bark creasing into peaks and troughs.

This is water striving for circularity. Blossom appearing in whorls, winged seeds swirling groundward. Currents cycle through xylem and phloem. Trees rise and fall in waves.

The sea has never been so far away.

And yet, in the deepest parts of the wood, there is something of a rock-pool stillness, something of the quiet of things submerged.

Down

The first time he'd fallen in the water it had been very quiet and very still. They had just come back from a long day out in the fields. Dark to dark up in the nacelles, shifting gear wheels and bedplates. The old man had been working him hard – waking him early and reeling off one job after another until there was no time to stop, or think, or do anything except climb, shift, repair and then return to the boat. The whole journey back the boy's arms and legs had been shaking. He had been smaller then, lighter, not much bigger than the old man. He hadn't been on the farm for long.

They'd pulled into the dock and the old man had gone ahead to fetch the charging cable, while the boy took the toolbag back to the storeroom. He didn't know exactly what happened. He still wasn't used to the movement of the boat and when he stepped onto the gangway it seemed to pitch. He stumbled and fell with the toolbag into the dock.

The weight dragged him down, but he didn't let go. These were their only tools – the old man had kept telling him that. If he lost or broke them then they wouldn't have anything. It didn't even cross the boy's mind to let go. He twisted, kicked out and sank deeper. The water got colder and there was no sound. He felt like he was moving very slowly and that the water was very thick. The grainy murk closed over him and the dock's strip lights disappeared.

He struggled. The weight of the bag pulled at him, but there was something else too. Even in the sheltered water of the dock he could feel the drag of the current sucking through the grilles beneath the gates. It was nothing really – barely more than a thread of energy, refracted and diffused – but it was the first time the boy had felt the power of the sea.

For a moment the storm was silent. The water closed around him like a blanket. Then it buoyed him up and he broke the surface and his ears crackled open in the full force of the wind.

Everything was dark. Everything was dark and he was sliding on the slope of a wave, but instead of slipping down he was moving up. The steeper the slope became, the higher he rose, until he was just below the tip. He was still holding on to the tow rope and he wrapped it round his wrist and gripped it as hard as he could, as the wave broke and drove downwards with the whole force of the storm behind it.

This time the water wasn't silent, but a roaring mass. The boy spun and tried to right himself, but the wave drove him deeper. The sea was white in every direction – there was no telling which way was up or down. He tried to kick, to drive with his arms, but he was rolling over and over. A space seemed to open below him and he dropped again, as though he was falling over a waterfall underwater. The weight above him was so vast he couldn't even straighten his body. Bubbles forced themselves from his nose and mouth, his chest burned, but still he was pushed deeper, through layers of light and dark until his back pressed against a solid surface and he knew there was nowhere else to go. He kicked down with his feet and they sank into the soft seabed. He tried to pull himself up the rope, but the force of water was too great. He thought, for a moment, how strange it would be to drown with his feet on land. Then, just when he thought he would have to gasp and take in a lungful of water, the pressure slackened and he felt the tug of the air.

He flailed, gasping to the surface, sucked in gulp after gulp. He shook the water from his eyes, tried to get his bearings. There was no sign of the maintenance boat, just the wind and rain in every direction. The tow rope trailed away into the dark. He tugged on it and felt resistance. His hands were numb and locked into fists. He forced them open and began to pull himself along the rope.

To his right, he felt the water rising again. He took a breath and dived under, swimming through the wave as far as he could, before coming up and hauling himself along the rope again. His head was numb and he was starting to shiver uncon-trollably. He had to keep moving, keep his blood pumping. He tried to kick his legs, but he couldn't feel them, or tell if they were even moving. All he could do was focus on his hands and keep hauling himself along.

He had to be nearing his boat, but he couldn't see anything through the rain. Suddenly the rope tightened and it was yanked through his hands. He splashed, grabbed and eventually forced his fingers to close, barely two feet from the end of the line. He shut his eyes, took a deep breath and began to pull himself along again.

The cold bit in deep, his muscles began to throb with a dull pain, and all he could think of was swinging one arm after the other, pulling himself inch by inch along the rope. The waves picked him up and dumped him down, dragged him left and right as if they were trying to split him apart. It became harder and harder to hold on, to will his fingers to open and close. His thoughts shrank back to the last warm cavities of his skull. He had barely the strength to push himself under when he saw the hull of the boat bearing down on him.

He twisted in the water, lifted his arms to shield his head and felt the rough metal bulk pressing down. He kicked, tried to pull himself further up the rope, but couldn't get out from under the mass of metal. The current was pushing against him, his lungs burned; there was nothing else to do. He let go of the rope, the current sucked him out, and he came up by the side of the boat.

He reached out, tried to find something to grab onto, but could only bang his numb hands against the metal before he was dragged away. He floated, caught his breath and tried to swim back, but a wave lifted the boat and he had to fight to stop himself being dragged under again. He could feel the side of the boat tilting above him. He reached up and at that moment a wave lifted him, slamming him into the hull. His body went limp and his vision shrank to a crackling grey tunnel. The wave pulled him back and flung him up once more. He landed hard on his stomach across the gunwale. His breath left him in a sharp gasp and he was about to slip back into the sea when his hand brushed against a cleat. His fingers closed and, somehow, he managed to hold on.

The boat tipped again. His feet dipped into the water. He held on with all his strength and, as the boat began to roll back the other way, he dragged himself up and onto the deck.

He opened his eyes and saw only rain and dark outlines. The wind screamed, sweeping itself across the sky like a trawling net. Still holding on to the cleat, he reached out and felt the corner of the cabin. Crawling on his stomach, not daring even to kneel, he worked his way along until he found the doorway. The door was open and banging every time the boat lurched. He grabbed hold of the bottom of the doorway, pulled himself in and kicked the door shut.

He dragged himself over to the steering column, wrapped his arms round it and closed his eyes.

At some point in the night the wind stopped screaming. At some point in the night the waves stopped pitching the boat at forty-five degrees. At some point in the night the boy must have fallen asleep, because when he opened his eyes again it was day.

He tried to lift his neck, but all he could manage was to turn his head to the side. He screwed his eyes shut, rolled over onto his stomach and pushed himself up onto his knees. His whole body was aching and the right side of his chest stabbed with pain each time he took a breath. His palms throbbed; there were patches where the skin had been rasped off and the flesh shone raw underneath. He reached carefully into his pocket for his watch, but it was gone.

He got up shakily and went over to the nearest window, then took a step back as the boat drifted a few metres from the biggest turbine he'd ever seen.

He leaned forward and looked up. It must have been a hundred and fifty metres to the nacelle. The jacket was almost as wide as the boat was long, the platform and railings high above the deck. All around, there were turbines of equal size rising like cliff-stacks into the sky, shifting their enormous blades in circuits of hundreds of metres. The cloud was not low, but the tips of the blades still disappeared in haze as they reached the tops of their arcs.

The boy had read about turbines like this in his technical manuals, but he'd never imagined he'd ever see them. These fields were the last of the farm to be built, back when they still built farms, but they had never been finished. They were hooked up to the grid, but the maintenance system and cameras had never been installed. The boy had often looked at them on the map and wondered what they were like, but their nearest edge was over eighty miles from the rig – well beyond the maintenance boat's range.

It was a bright day and the wind was blowing clean and consistent. The turbines swept their gleaming blades in and out of the clouds. The boy couldn't take his eyes off them.

A wave washed back from a nearby jacket, rocking the boat. There was a hollow clang from somewhere in the hull and the deck pitched at an angle and stayed there.

The boy looked out at the deck, strewn with rope and tarpaulin. He looked around the cabin, at the steering column, the useless ignition switch, the empty hole where the satnav and the tracker should be. There was another clang from the hull. He was over eighty miles from the rig, in a listing boat with a broken engine. He looked up as he drifted past another turbine. He had to stop moving.

He went into the cabin and tested the steering. It worked. The boat was sluggish, but it worked. He could get in close to a tower, but he'd need a way of catching hold of the jacket. Then he saw the tow-line, still hanging from the bow of the boat.

He took the hook from one of the mooring cables and attached it to the end of the tow-line. He had to work just with his fingers, keeping any pressure off his raw palms. He kept dropping the rope as he tried to coil it, but eventually he managed to get everything ready.

In the cabin, he lined the boat up, so it would drift near to the next turbine, then he locked the wheel and went back on deck. The turbine loomed in close. He lined up his shot, tested the weight of the hook and threw it up at the jacket.

The hook flew straight at the rail, then dipped at the last minute and fell into the water. The coil had tangled and caught on the gunwale. The boy grabbed the rope and hauled it back in. The rope scraped against his palms and they started bleeding. He pulled down his sleeves to cover them and carried on hauling. The boat drifted slowly on. When he had the hook on deck he untangled the coil. The boat passed the end of the jacket. The boy lifted the hook, quickly took aim and flung it as hard as he could. The hook went over the rail, bounced off the tower and landed on the platform. As the boat drifted on, the remaining rope unravelled slowly from the deck. Then, when it had reached its limit, the hook rose up from the platform and scraped along the top of the rail. The boy watched, the boat drifted, the hook scraped, wobbled and caught on the junction with one of the uprights. The rope tightened. The boat turned a slow arc. The rope quivered. The boat stilled.

The boy sat down heavily on the deck. He could feel his muscles beginning to seize up. He had to pull himself in to the tower. He had to get properly moored. He had to check the engine, he had to … He looked around at his useless boat, then down at his useless, bloodied hands. He ran through the list again. He had to get properly moored, he had to check something, he had to … He clenched his fists and gasped at the pain in his hands, then flinched at the pain in his ribs.

His thoughts surged again. He had to check things, he had to get things secure, he had to … The other boat. The boy stared straight ahead across the deck. The old man. The old man was still on the other boat. What had happened? He tried to think back. They'd had a fight. The storm had hit. When he'd left the cabin, the old man had been sitting in the corner holding on to the strap. He'd looked at the boy. He'd said something. What was it? The boy tried to think, but all he could remember was the wind blasting into the cabin, the door slamming open and closed. He felt a tightness grip his chest and throat and he almost retched, spitting up a mouthful of seawater.

How much charge had been left at the end? He closed his eyes, tried to remember the control panel, the number on the gauge. But as soon as he did so, he saw the storm – the toppling waves, the sideways spray. He could feel the pull of the water on his limbs, the weight and the pressure of it.

He opened his eyes and tried to think but he was so tired. He needed to rest. He closed his eyes again. The waves towered over him. The weight and pressure pulled at him. He lay down on the deck. Maybe he should just stay here for a while. It would be easier to just stay here and rest. He didn't need to open his eyes. The deck was almost comfortable. He felt almost warm. Maybe he didn't need to move any more.

He'd tried to get the toolbag up on top of him and push it back up through the murky water of the dock, but he was too weak. He sank lower. The current coming under the gates tugged at his feet.

A shadow wavered above him – a dark shape that appeared and disappeared in the ripples. The boy reached up, made a last grasp for the surface, then felt the hard metal of a boathook. He grabbed it and held on as he was hauled up through the water.

He came up to the surface retching, kicked, and then, with the last of his strength, made it to the ladder.

Rough hands grabbed the toolbag from him, then reached down, took hold of his collar and dragged him up onto the gangway.

'Why the hell did you keep hold of that bag?' The old man's voice was hoarse.

The boy didn't answer. He lay down on the gangway and didn't move. He felt almost warm. He was so tired. The days had been so long, the work had been so hard. Maybe it would be easier to just stay there and rest. He closed his eyes. Water dripped off his clothes and fell like rain through the grille.

'Get up.'

The boy opened his eyes slowly. The old man was standing over him. His arms were crossed and his voice echoed off the dock's walls. The boy wished he would stop talking so loudly and leave him for a moment, let him rest – he wouldn't be long; it was just that he was so comfortable. The water down there had been so quiet and so still.

The old man didn't reach down to him. He kept his arms folded tight across his chest. 'Get up now,' he said.

Up

Inside, the turbine felt even bigger. From the bottom, the gantry where the tower met the nacelle wasn't even visible. The pallid wall lights grew smaller and then vanished from sight. It was like staring up a mineshaft that had been cut out of the sky. Every sound echoed up the tower and came back down a few moments later, strange and distorted.

The wind gusted through the open doorway. The boy was still soaking and he was starting to shiver again. It had taken a long time to pull the boat in. He'd torn strips off the bed sheets and wrapped them round his hands, but his palms were still throbbing. It was late in the day and it would be getting cold soon. He had to get up to the nacelle, get dry and warm, then try and figure out where he was, what to do.

He pressed the button for the service lift, but nothing happened. He pressed it again. Nothing. The turbine had power – its lights were on and he'd seen its blades turning. It just didn't have a working lift. The boy closed his eyes and tried

146

to rub some life back into his freezing limbs. Of all the turbines he could have picked … He tried to order his thoughts, which grated like sea ice in his skull. He couldn't risk casting off again. Even if he managed to hook onto another turbine, there was no guarantee that its lift would be working either. He considered going back to the boat or just staying at the bottom of the tower. No, if he didn't get up into the nacelle before nightfall, he'd freeze. He looked up the tower and at the narrow service ladder that rose, parallel to the lift shaft, up the sheer and tapering wall. At least it would warm him up.

The boy had climbed turbines before, but nothing of this scale. The ladder was standard size, which meant four rungs per metre. Which meant … which meant a lot of rungs. When he looked up, the horizontal lines began to judder, so he stopped looking up. He reached out and took hold of a rung. Next to the ladder there was a bright yellow panel giving detailed instructions on the correct usage of a safety harness and slider. The boy looked down at his cloth-bound hands. He waited a moment, stretched his neck, then started to climb.

After the first twenty rungs his hands had seized up and blood was trickling down his wrists and up his sleeves. He couldn't get a proper grip, so he started hooking one forearm over the rung to hold himself in place and using only one hand to reach up at a time. It slowed his pace, but it kept him stable and gradually he made his way, rung after rung, reaching up, hooking his arm and bringing his feet up after him. Ten rungs with one arm, then ten with the other.

Fifty rungs. Sixty. Below him, the base of the tower had receded to a small disc, but up above, the nacelle seemed no closer.

A hundred rungs and his legs were starting to shake, whichever arm he hooked over the rung would quickly cramp up, his hands were slick with sweat and the cloth was starting to come loose. Twice already he'd slipped – one arm and leg swinging out into space. The tapering of the tower was barely a few degrees, but as the boy climbed higher it felt like he was hanging almost upside down. He slowed his pace, made sure of his grip, kept going.

His neck was aching from looking up, so he stared straight ahead as he climbed. There were no horizontal rivet lines on the tower, which meant that each side must have been manufactured as a single piece. It was the sort of thing the boy would normally have found interesting.

Somewhere around two hundred rungs he lost count, but eventually he reached up and felt the edge of a gantry. In his relief he almost lost the strength to pull himself up. He lay face down on the grille and closed his eyes. His muscles were burning and his mouth and throat were so dry he could hardly swallow. He had drunk a few mouthfuls of brackish water from the container on the boat. He should have gone back for more before he started climbing. Why hadn't he gone back for more?

It was okay. He'd get the lift working and then he would go back down. He was sure he could get the lift working. There was power, so it had to just be a connection. He took a deep breath and pushed himself up, but the hatch to the nacelle wasn't there. Instead, the ladder carried on, as far as he could see, up into the gloom. On the wall next to him there was a cross-section diagram of the tower, highlighting the first of two evenly spaced service platforms, installed to give workers a rest during their climb.

The boy sat at the top of the tower. His legs were shaking, his hands were numb, his arms and back burning. He was drenched in sweat and the cold was setting in again.

For the last hundred rungs all he'd heard in his footsteps, in his breathing, in the throbbing of his hands, was the rhythm of the old man's words: 'The storm's … coming … back … You're as … stupid … as … he was.'

However he'd tried to vary his movements, the rhythm stayed the same, until all he could do was listen and climb and, when he got to the top, wait until his heart rate slowed.

He swallowed gratingly and pushed himself to his feet, staggered, then steadied himself against the rail. He looked up at the hatch. At least it wasn't rusted shut. He reached up, even though it felt as if his arms wouldn't reach, and pushed, even though it felt as if he couldn't push. The hatch opened and he climbed up into the nacelle.

The lights came on automatically and the boy found himself standing in the middle of a spacious room surrounded by vast components all encased in white. At first he thought the machinery wasn't working, then he realized it was just so quiet he could barely hear it. On the far side of the room there was a gleaming control panel and attached to the housings of every piece of machinery were coloured signs detailing design specs, efficiency ratings and safety warnings.

The boy went over to where the gearbox should have been, but instead the drive shaft connected straight to the generator. 'Direct drive,' he said. He'd read about the system before. They had fewer moving parts, increased efficiency. He started to open the casing, to get inside and see how it worked, but then he stopped and looked around. He'd forgotten for a moment where he was, what had happened. He rubbed his hand over his jaw. What was he supposed to be doing? It took him a while to remember the control panel – he was meant to be finding that and fixing the lift, and then going back down to get water.

The lift was easy to fix. In fact, it didn't need fixing; it just needed its circuits switching on. By the look of things, no one had touched anything since the turbine had been installed. There were plastic films over all of the buttons, and instruction booklets in plastic holders next to every piece of machinery. The boy picked one up, felt its untouched pages and uncracked spine. Then he noticed, just beyond the control panel, another door.

It wasn't heavy like a hatch; it was just a normal door. The boy took hold of the handle and opened it slowly, half-expecting there to be nothing but open air beyond; but instead there was another room, the same size as the one housing the turbine's workings.

Automatic lights flickered on, revealing a long table and six black chairs wrapped in cellophane. On one wall there was a large screen, covered in a layer of bubble-wrap, and on the other walls there were framed posters – technical drawings of turbines and gearboxes, pictures of the farm on clear bright days with words like 'future', 'stability' and 'security' printed on them. In the far corner of the room there were more posters, rolled up and leaning against a wall, and a stack of cardboard boxes.

The boy took a step forward, then stopped, lifted one foot then the other. The floor looked strange. He leaned down slowly, took his boots and socks off, working loose the stiff laces, and let his bare feet press into the fibres of the clean grey carpet.

He walked into the room and turned around. There was a tall, rectangular machine behind the door. It looked like a water filter. On one side there was a clear plastic tube filled with paper cups. The boy went over, pulled out a cup and placed it beneath the spout. He found a switch on the side and turned it on. The machine whirred and groaned. There was a hissing and a juddering of pipes, then a row of buttons lit up and the machine settled to a low electrical hum. The boy pressed the top button.

There was a rumble and a loud hiss and steam began venting from the machine. The boy pressed the button again, but the machine carried on. He took a step back. A smell like burning filled the room. He was about to pull the plug out of the wall, when the machine stopped and the lights on the buttons came back on. He stepped forward and peered into his cup. It was full of steaming, black liquid.

The buttons had strips of protective tape next to them. He unpeeled the tape slowly from the button he'd pressed, revealing a label.

'Coffee?' he said.

He picked up the cup and touched the liquid to his mouth. It was scalding and caused his salt-cracked lips to sting. It tasted almost bitter, almost burnt. He waited, then took another sip and felt the hot liquid work its way down into his body. It crossed his mind that the old man would like it. He had talked about something once – something he used to drink that tasted bitter and strong. Maybe it was coffee. He had tried to describe it to the boy but the boy had been replacing a fuse and hadn't really been listening.

He looked around, at the table, the chairs, the pictures of this strange, pristine farm covering the walls. Everything gleamed. Everything was too bright.

The boy closed his eyes. Waves towered over him. The door of the cabin swung in the storm. The battery gauge shone, but no numbers were visible. He opened his eyes, pushed it all down until it settled tightly in his chest. He couldn't think of it.

He stood there for a long time. Finally, he put his cup down on the table and went back into the other room, over to the roof hatch. He pressed a button and the hatch opened, flooding the nacelle with wind and noise. He climbed the ladder and looked out. The wind roared around him, shaking the hatch, which he sheltered behind. The roof of the nacelle was huge; there was a small helipad in front of the hatch. It took the boy a moment to catch his breath and fully open his eyes. He was so high. It felt like he was balancing in the centre of a great disc of water. Behind him and to either side the turbines spread in straight rows, shrinking over and beyond the sea's curving limit. But straight ahead, eastwards, there were ten rows and then nothing. The boy closed his eyes and opened them again. The wind boomed across the water. There was the edge of the farm and, beyond it, the open sea.

c.11,000 Before Present

One day a coastline appears – a band of silver stretching across the horizon – and suddenly there is an edge to things.

The forest thins and turns to salt marsh, which turns to mudflats and tidal lagoons. Rivers become brackish and undrinkable. They spread into estuaries, which shift with each tide into a mesh of furrows, sandbanks and channels.

What yesterday was sure footing is now unstable ground.

Crusts of sand loosen and slip. Drought turns to flood, heat to searing cold, silence to cacophony. Plants drift from pool to pool like animals; animals take root and bloom like flowers. The water teems with brittle shells; and within each shell is a soft, watery body.

*

The tide presses in and draws back. It presses in a little more, it draws back a little less, each day. Low cliffs calve boulders. Boulders fracture into rocks. Rocks are ground down to pebbles. The sea rises by a pebble's breadth each year.

Suddenly there is an edge to things. What yesterday was sure footing is now unstable ground.

Paper Cups

The boy stood in the roof hatch with an armful of paper cups. He'd thought it was well into the day, but when he opened the hatch he found it was still dark – the sky just beginning to leach a dull red from far out across the sea. He must have been awake all night. He looked down. There were paper cups covering every surface of the nacelle, spilling over onto the floor. He had no idea how long he'd been out there.

The sky turned rusty, then grey, then settled on a yellowish tint that seemed to glow through the thinner patches of cloud like a torch shining through a sheet. He dropped the cups over the side of the nacelle, one by one.

On the first day he stayed up in the tower. He couldn't bring himself to go back down and see the state of his boat.

He checked the control panel and the screen in the back room to see if they were connected up to the system. He thought that if he could access a map of the farm, he might be able to find out where exactly he was; but, while all the electrics in the turbine were working, none of it was linked up to the system.

He sat at the table in one of the cellophane-covered chairs and retied the ragged cloths around his palms. He was too tired to move or sleep. He reached over for the stack of boxes in the corner of the room.

Three of them were full of brochures and information leaflets – piles of them, all exactly the same, with the same pictures that were on the walls, and the same words, just more of them. The last box was much lighter. At first the boy thought it was empty, but when he opened it he found it contained hundreds more paper cups for the coffee machine. They had some kind of image printed on the side. It wasn't the Company logo, yet it seemed familiar. The boy sat and stared at it for a long time, but could not place it exactly.

That first night he tried to sleep, but when he closed his eyes all he saw were the towering waves, the empty cabin, the door slamming open and closed in the wind. He got up, drank coffee, and failed to sleep again.

The damage to the boat was as bad as he'd expected. The engine had come loose from its housing and been smashed apart as it was thrown around the hull. The heaviest parts and three of the batteries had finally come to rest on the port side of the engine room, causing the boat to list. The hull, at least, seemed intact, although the remains of the engine were sitting in over a foot of water that sloshed in the bottom of the keel.

The boy drained it by hand, which took most of the day, working back and forth with a small plastic bucket. By the time he'd finished, it was almost dark. Not that he needed any light to see what he knew already – what remained of the engine was irreparable.

There was nothing of use in the nacelle. The turbine's components were all in sealed units. According to the technical posters, this made each part easier to replace. It also meant that the boy had no idea how they worked.

He sat at the table and folded his hands together. The wind buffeted the walls of the nacelle. He was miles from the rig, miles from anywhere, moored to a turbine with a boat that he had no way of fixing. Just like his father.

Except that what the boy had done was worse.

The wind thumped and groaned. Sometimes it sounded like footsteps at the bottom of the tower; sometimes like the creak of boots out on the deck of the boat.

* * *

He took the roll-mat and sheets from the cabin, gathered together the few tools he had left in the engine room, unloaded the crates from the hold and, cramming them into the small service lift, took them up to the top of the tower.

He laid the roll-mat down in a corner of the inner room and stacked the crates against the far wall. There were enough supplies to last for months. The food in the tins was fine, but the damp of the hold had caused most of the labels to lose their adhesion and slip into a brown pulp at the bottom of the crates.

The tins had been stored on the boat for so long that their edges were covered in a rind of rust. The sheet was speckled with pale brown spots of damp, and the roll-mat, when he laid it flat, crumbled away at the edges. Bits of foam broke off and stuck to the damp on the boy's hands.

He ate something that sounded like fruit, but had the bitter tang of melted plastic; something that rattled like plastic, but tasted sickly sweet.

He sat in the cellophane-wrapped chair for hours. He found that, if he sat still for too long, a day could pass by without him really even noticing it.

Some days he would go down the tower to check on the boat. He would test the moorings, examine the hull and measure the level of the water that had crept back in overnight.

Some days he would stay in the nacelle and read through every identical leaflet in the boxes, drinking cup after cup of coffee.

* * *

Whenever he looked at the logo on the cups, he started humming a tune. He tried to place it, but as soon as he tried to focus, it evaporated from his mind. He tried to stop himself humming it, but it would creep back before he realized what he was doing.

The boat wallowed in the water, listing and scoured with rain. It looked almost the same now as the night he'd found it – the same broken engine, the same objects strewn over the deck. He thought about his father's tools, which he'd found around the engine, and the blown panel in the transformer – up until the end his father had been trying to make the boat work.

He wondered, for a moment, what anyone would find of him. Nothing but a crumpled bed at the top of the tower, some empty tins, a pile of used paper cups.

He tidied the deck of the boat, went down into the engine room and gathered together his father's tools, then he climbed up onto the jacket and sat, watching the water, scanning it for anything that might drift past, anything he could use. Anything.

The water buckled and creased. A shadow moved across the surface, as if there was someone just behind him. He didn't turn around. After a while he felt the platform give a little, as if someone had shifted their weight.

* * *

He'd been sitting, staring out at the water, for so long that he almost didn't notice when he did see something. At first it looked like a long pole, but as it drifted closer, he saw that one end was broad and flat. It was a paddle, half eaten away by the sea, but it was still a paddle.

He rushed down to the boat, grabbed the tow-line, then climbed back up to the jacket and scanned the water again. He waited until the paddle was as close as it would get, then he threw the hook. It hit the shaft, but there was nothing to catch onto, so it slipped off. He pulled the line back in and tried again, but the same thing happened.

He stood for a moment, watching as the paddle drifted further on, then he took off his boots, tied one end of the tow-line to the railing and the other round his waist, and jumped into the water.

He swam as hard as he could, but the current was strong and the paddle was being dragged away quickly. He took another three strokes. It was almost in reach. Then the line tightened and jerked him to a stop. He yanked it and reached out again, but the paddle was metres away. He strained on the line, then felt the knot slip. He froze. The current was grasping at his legs, trying to pull him out. Slowly and carefully, already shivering, he took hold of the line and pulled himself back to the tower.

* * *

Every night he climbed to the roof hatch and looked out, searching for any light, for any sign of anything. He would stand there for hours, sheltering behind the hatch, gripping a cup of coffee against the cold.

Sometimes he would think he'd seen a glimmer, but it would just be the lights from inside the nacelle reflecting off the water that streamed from his eyes as he stood, staring into the wind.

Then, once, he did see something, just as he was turning to go back inside – a tiny light, moving slowly far out to sea. His heart started drumming hard. He waved with both arms and shouted until his voice went hoarse; but the dark pressed in and the wind dragged away any sound.

He stood with his hands on the rim of the hatch and, as the cold crept up through the metal, he remembered what the light was. His father had told him about them once, long ago. He had lifted the boy up to a tiny window and the boy had gripped the metal sill and they had watched a light travelling through the dark. It was a cargo ship – a boat the size of a town, hauling tonnes of supplies around the world. His father had pointed out of the window and told him how they used to travel in great convoys, how the docks would be jammed all year round. How there were hardly any left now, maybe just one or two a year, still travelling along the shipping lanes, like the last of their species still following the old migratory routes.

* * *

The boy removed one of the interior lights from the wall of the nacelle, extended the wiring and stood in the roof hatch, pointing it out into the dark. He stood there, night after night, but he never saw the light again.

He read through every technical manual in the nacelle. The components and systems were unfamiliar, but if he could take out the right parts, he thought there might be a way of making a whole new engine for the boat.

He stayed up for three full days, drinking coffee and making plans, scribbling notes, calculations and diagrams over the backs of the posters. It was only when he had almost finished that he realized he hadn't checked the scale of the original drawings – the components he'd been reading about were only a few centimetres long.

He made the motor anyway, connected it to the main supply and watched as it burned itself out, leaving a small black mark in the middle of the table.

He found that if he drank three coffees his hands would shake. If he drank four, his eyelids would begin to quiver. If he drank five, everything settled back down to how it was before.

* * *

He took apart the turbine's control panel and put it back together again. With the sealed components it took no time. So he removed one of the components, broke it open and laid the contents out over the table.

From the other room he heard the whine of the blade controls, which sounded like a panel being opened, and the steady clicks of the cooling generator, which could have been machine parts being laid out carefully on the floor.

It took him all day to put the component back together again, but when he reinserted it, it had stopped working.

The floor of the nacelle was covered with broken and disman-tled parts. The boy sat among them, a cup of coffee on his right side and a pile of empty tins on his left. He took one of the empty tins and laid it down in front of him. Then he got his knife and started to cut a slit down one side.

He cut slowly and carefully, working each piece until he had a base and a stand. He fixed the base to the stand, then he took the rest of the tin and cut three long, curved shapes from it.

He worked hard at making the edges as smooth as possible. When they were all cut he twisted the ends together into a narrow spindle.

He pressed the spindle into a hole in the stand, then held up the model turbine and blew gently. The blades turned. Their edges were sharp and glinted in the light.

He got up, placed the turbine carefully on the table and made himself another coffee. On his way to the machine, he began humming the beginning of a tune. He tried to remember the rest, but it slipped away.

It turned out that the coffee machine could be made to dispense water too, which the boy only found out after his hands shook so much that he pushed the wrong button.

Sleep finally came – a deep and total sleep, thick as engine grease, shutting out all sound and sensation.

The boy did not dream of waves. He dreamed that he was moving down a tunnel. No, not a tunnel, down a corridor, the main corridor of the rig. There was the rec room up ahead. He walked to the door and stopped. Everything was new. There were sofas and pictures on the walls, the pool table with both cues and all its pockets intact. He turned and looked into the conference room – there was a large screen on the wall-bracket, chairs round the table. He could hear the wind thumping on the outer walls, but then he realized that it was just his own heart thumping, very slowly and distantly. So slow in fact that, between each beat, he was able to pace out every level of the rig.

Everything was working. There were no holes in the floor panels, no leaks, no patches of rust. When he passed the control room he saw brand-new computers whirring softly.

Down in the dock there was a boat. It was clean and freshly painted. The boy climbed on board, started the engine and left the dock.

He travelled through the farm, passing row after row until he could see, in the distance, the open sea. He pushed on the power lever and the engine silently accelerated. It was only then that he heard it – a dripping sound coming from below.

He cut the engine, opened the hatch and climbed down into the dark. He stepped quietly over the battery and the prop shaft. Then he felt a drip on his shoulder. He looked up – there was a crack in the hull. It dripped again. He reached up and touched the crack and it widened, turned to a trickle, then a steady stream. He reached up with two hands, tried to plug the gap, but the water kept coming.

He was soaked through in seconds. There was water in his eyes, in his mouth. He looked down – his toolbag was near the far wall. He let go of the crack with one hand and the metal creaked. He put his hand back and tried to reach his toolbag with his foot, but it was too far. The water was spreading all around him now. He spat it out and was about to shout for help, when he saw, through the blur of water, someone standing, looking down into the hatch.

The shape wavered – appearing and disappearing in the ripples. His face and features were obscured. All that was visible was his overall shape: he was tall, standing very upright and still. He stood there, watching.

The boy tried to shout, tried to say something, but all that came out was a kind of bubbling, a kind of gurgling. He held on to the leak, blinking through the spray as the water spread around his feet and began pooling in the hold.

The figure just stood there, raised his hand and rubbed the side of his jaw.

When the boy finally woke, he had no idea how many days he'd been out. And he didn't care; because all he could think of was his pounding headache and all he could do was stagger to the machine, pour himself a coffee and wait for the pain to subside.

He blew on the tin turbine but the blades wedged together. He tried to untangle them but they bent sideways, folding in on themselves like fingers grasping the air.

He sat at the table, surrounded by turbine components, empty tins, leaflets, posters and used paper cups.

Below him the yaw system clacked and droned; above him the wind thudded against the tower.

For a moment it sounded like footsteps and he sat upright, listening. But as the boy listened the steps slowly faded and disappeared, like the cargo ship's light slipping away over the horizon, like when he'd sat in that small room with the rows of orange chairs and tried to say something, tried to call out, but his father had already turned and gone, his boots echoing away down the corridor.

Or maybe it was like the shapes he'd pulled out of the old man's nets, which dissolved into grit and ran down his hands, which were never really anything, which were never really there at all.

The tune came into his head again, tinny and repetitive. The boy looked down at the paper cups, then he stood up, gathered together an armful and took them to the roof hatch.

He dropped the last paper cup off the top of the tower. It sank; then, one by one, the cups rose back on an up-draught and scattered across the sky. He watched them for a moment as they wheeled away, then he closed the hatch and climbed back down into the nacelle.

Fish

The boy lifted the tin and turned it in the light. It was exactly the same as all of the others, except there was a small fragment of label still clinging to the bottom edge. There was something tiny written on it that he couldn't make out, and a faded picture of a fish. He placed it on the table in front of him and sat back in the chair.

The cellophane creaked. The sound grated and the shiny surfaces grated but he didn't move or get up. He'd stopped going outside. He'd stopped watching the water for things that might drift past. He'd stopped searching for lights. He'd stopped going down to check on the boat. For a long time, all he'd done was stare out at the horizon – the long, uninterrupted line of it. The openness almost made him dizzy. There was nothing to draw the eye, nothing to catch hold of, just the clouds rushing past, and the currents sweeping. Everything moved away from him out there – as soon as he tried to see what the clouds were doing they shifted and changed shape, the currents turned and backed away. The horizon was all there was. He'd stood and stared at it for so long that his eyes had started to ache and a thin line had appeared wherever he looked. So he'd stopped looking.

He studied the tiny picture of the fish. The last nine tins he'd eaten had all been exactly the same – some sort of pale jelly with chunks of a foamy substance suspended in it. He had no idea what it was, or even what it really tasted like any more.

He'd tried choosing tins from other crates, tins that sounded different, tins that varied in weight; but each time he opened them up, there was the pale jelly, the foamy chunks, waiting.

He picked up the tin opener and cut into the top of the tin. It wasn't jelly, but it wasn't anything else recognizable either. The boy dug in with the end of the tin opener and took a small mouthful. He didn't think it tasted like fish, but then he couldn't remember what fish tasted like. Maybe all of these tins were fish. Maybe that's what he'd been eating all along.

He thought about the days, the years, he'd spent setting and checking his line. He'd never caught a fish. He'd never even seen a fish. But every day he'd gone down to the rig's support to check his line. Why had he done it? He must have thought, at some point, that he would catch something. What was it called, that feeling? He couldn't remember.

* * *

It was the first time the supply boat was late – that's when he'd started.

The supplies had got lower and lower. Days had passed with no sign of the boat on the screens.

The old man had told him not to worry. 'Do you know how many stages there are in the supply chain?' he said. 'Do you know how far one tin has to travel to get to us out here?' He was lounging on the sofa in the rec room, throwing pool balls at an empty mug on the table in front of him. He kept missing and the balls hit the table with a dull *thonk*, leaving shallow indents in the laminate. 'Think about it.' *Thonk*. 'The food's grown in the vats, then has to travel across the interior to the processors …' *thonk* '… then on to the canneries on the coast. It goes from cannery to testing centre …' *thonk* '… to distribution centre, then dock.' *Thonk*. 'And at every stage it has to pass through the hands of someone like the fat man, who wants to take his or her share.'

A ball glanced the mug, which began to wobble then tilt in wider arcs until it fell onto its side and rolled off the table. 'That counts,' the old man said. He stretched back into the sofa. 'So really,' he said, 'we should be glad that anything gets here at all.'

'Yeah,' the boy had said. Then he'd gone and found some old bent screws, tied them to a piece of rope and started fishing.

There were still almost a hundred tins left. There had to be one somewhere that tasted of something. The boy reached into the crate, took out another, opened it, tasted it and then put it on

171

the table next to the first one. He took out another tin and did the same thing.

Soon there were six tins standing on the table. He hadn't even been able to bring himself to taste the last few. He sat back and the cellophane creaked again, louder this time. He tried to stop moving. That was six days' worth of food he'd just wasted. Six fewer days that he'd be able to last out there.

He leaned forward and opened another tin. Might as well make it an even week. He could open up all of those tins. He could just take all of the crates and push them off the top of the nacelle. That, at least, would settle things.

What would happen if the supply boat didn't turn up? That's what the boy had wanted to know. They were down to their last crate of food and still there was no sign. He checked the screens every day. He logged the delay with the system but all he got back was an automated message thanking him for his input.

What if the boat had sunk? What if their supplies had been delivered somewhere else by mistake? What if there was a fault in the system and they'd been forgotten? What would happen …?

'What do you think will happen?' was all the old man said.

So the boy tried to talk about rationing. If they only ate half a tin a day, it would give them a few extra weeks. If they went down to a third, they'd last over a month.

Eventually, the old man got so annoyed that he went into the galley, took all the tins out of the crate and divided them into two piles. 'There,' he said. 'You can do what you bloody want with yours.'

A few days later the boy found him using a tin of vegetables to patch up a crack in one of the air vents. 'Couldn't find the putty,' was all the old man said.

A dull ache started to spread up and press at the front of the boy's skull. He closed his eyes and rubbed at his temples. He needed a coffee. If there had been a clock up in the nacelle, he could have set it by the regularity of these headaches.

He got up and went over to the machine. He put a cup in and pressed the button. The machine gurgled, hissed and dispensed a slightly tinted liquid, the colour of water from a rusty pipe. The boy picked up the cup, sniffed it, then put it down on the floor and got another one. The machine did the same thing again. He hit the side panel and jabbed at the button. A small red light came on. He stood looking at the machine for a long time, then he left the room.

He went up to the roof hatch and climbed out. There was a strange mugginess in the air, as if it had grown thicker. The clouds had turned lumpy and dull, like old mattresses. It wasn't warm – he couldn't remember what warm air was like – but the thickness of the air, the sluggishness, almost made it seem warm. Even the wind seemed heavier, as if it were slumping over the turbines, muffling the sound of the blades.

Behind him one of the turbine's blades ground out an enormous arc, raised itself to vertical and then slowly began to fall.

The boy climbed up onto the roof of the nacelle, held on to the top of the hatch to steady himself and slid his feet towards the edge. He stood there, swaying in the wind. The blades behind him rose and then fell. He sat down, pulled his knees up to his chest and laid his head on his arms.

He'd been checking the satellite map every day, staring at the screen for hours, willing the supply boat to appear. He sat in the control room, blinking himself awake. He knew he should just get up and do something, but whenever he thought about it the screen would flicker and he would lean in closer, certain he had seen something move across the map. Then his head would droop and he'd blink himself awake. He'd taken to eating barely a quarter of a tin a day.

Still the old man seemed to think it was fine. He kept on wasting food – leaving half-eaten tins standing around on the side in the galley, the tops going dark and crusty until there was nothing the boy could do except throw them away. He even thought it would be funny to tie a tin to the end of the boy's fishing line. The boy had quickly hauled it in when he felt the weight, then realized what it was and wordlessly returned it to the old man's store.

The old man started to gamble with their remaining food. He would bet a tin that he could pot every ball on the table with the snapped cue; or that he could unravel, and then re-coil, the fire hose quicker than the boy. It was always something stupid and if the boy took the bet he almost always won.

When the connection to the central system went down the old man had bet three tins that the boy couldn't fix it before the supply boat came back. The signal was still coming in to the rig, so it had to be a problem with the wiring. The boy wasn't going to do it, but without access to the system he couldn't check the satellite map – he'd have no way of knowing when the boat would arrive.

In the end it took seven days. A week of taking up floor panels, testing connections and following cables through the bowels of the rig. It turned out that one of the wires had snapped. It was a clean break and easy enough to fix with a connecting box. But it was a strange way for the connection to go down. The boy had never known it to happen before or since. Still, he took the tins from the old man, who didn't seem to care.

It was almost strange, feeling the skin of his face against the skin of his arms. He couldn't picture himself, couldn't disassociate himself from the heaviness of the air. The tiredness was so deep that the boy could hear his brain creaking like the cellophane on the chair. His hands and arms felt very far away, even though he could smell the tins on his fingers, and feel the dent in his palm from where he must have been clenching the handle of the tin opener.

He tried to open his eyes, but they were too heavy to open properly, so he left them half-closed. The blades rose and fell behind him. They sounded very far away.

* * *

When the supply boat finally turned up, the boy had won so many bets off the old man that he still had a cupboard-full of tins and had been back to eating one a day.

He'd forgotten that. He'd always remembered his relief when the boat had arrived, the way he'd tracked it as it blinked across the map, but he'd forgotten about how easily he'd won those bets. He'd forgotten about the wire too – how clean the break had been, as if it had been cut carefully with a knife.

And there was something else he'd forgotten: how he'd gone into the galley after the pilot had left and seen the old man cramming down a tin of protein as if he hadn't eaten in days, leaning over the counter, his eyes closed, waiting for the stomach cramps to subside.

The boy sat up. He'd been thinking about the wire, the cleanness of the cut. It was perfectly straight, like the lines of the towers, like the line in the water. He rubbed over his eyes. There was a line in the water. A few rows to the north. As he watched, it juddered, buckled, seemed to shift closer. He closed his eyes and opened them again.

'Who's cut the sea in two?' he said. His own voice startled him.

There was something different about the water. It wasn't just his eyes. He got up quickly, too quickly. He swayed, then gripped hold of the top of the hatch. His heart started to hammer in his throat. A few rows to the north he could see a line stretching from east to west, dividing the entire sea. On the south side of the line the water was the same murky grey it always was, but on the north it looked different. As he watched, the line moved further south, until it swept past his turbine, bringing with it the clearest water he'd ever seen. It was so clear that, even from the top of the turbine, he could see right down to the seabed. He could see the jacket foundations, the underwater cables, and he could also make out shapes floating through the farm.

They looked like plastic bags – a whole container-load of plastic bags. They were all the same colour and they rose and sank in the same strange way that plastic bags did. But they were different sizes and, now the boy looked harder, he could see that they were shoaling together and none were catching on the turbines as they passed. They made the water look dense, almost like the jelly in the tins. There were so many of them, they were spreading out across the water as far as he could see.

He raced to the lift, got to the bottom of the tower, ran outside and leaned over the rails of the jacket, staring down into the strange, clear waters. At first he couldn't see anything except the way the dull light seemed to glint down towards the seabed. A twist of plastic floated past, then an orange net. He waited. Still nothing happened. Another twist of plastic swept past. He turned round, thought he must have miscalculated, that he'd missed them, but then they appeared.

They were vast, clear globes, like planets, with pale stems, or legs, or something, trailing down from them. He could see their veins in purple rings, circling their bodies and spreading down, as if a line of paint had been spilled. Their inner workings were right there – the strange purple and orange wires of them, their circuits, their entire systems that looked too delicate for the huge, silent creatures that were sweeping in. They came one by one at first, then in their tens, then hundreds, massing in the water like drops of oil, until it seemed like there were more of them than there was water. They swelled and pulsed like heartbeats, as they drifted slowly past on the currents.

One bumped against the hull of the boat. The boy scrambled down the ladder, picked up a bucket and untied one of the ropes holding the bundle of tarpaulin down. He looped the rope through the handle of the bucket and ran back to the gunwale, but the one next to the boat had gone. It must have sunk down, dipped under the hull and then carried on away with the rest.

The boy stood watching as they drifted past. It was amazing how easily they moved, using the currents, flexing, tilting, as though being driven on by some underwater breeze.

Another one drifted closer and he was about to throw the bucket, but then he stopped. Out of the corner of his eye he saw the loose tarpaulin flapping on the deck. He lowered his arm and watched as the sheet ballooned up and slumped back down. He turned back to look again at the creatures, their bodies swelling as they moved through the sea. He went over to the tarpaulin, lifted up one corner and felt the tug of the wind.

Westerlies

Everything was laid out on the deck – poles, ropes, tools and the tarpaulin. The boy stood by the cabin and studied them. He went over to the tarp and lifted up one edge, stretching it out. The wind caught it and it flapped and buckled, then a sudden gust tore it from his hands and almost sent it flying overboard. He grabbed it, folded it carefully, placing the poles across it to weigh it down, and then went back to standing by the cabin.

The tarp would need to be secured at the corners, to allow the centre to catch the wind. There were reinforced eyelets running down two of the edges. If he threaded the ropes through them, he could tighten or loosen them to adjust the size of the sheet. Then he would just need some kind of frame to give it structure and hold the tarp in place.

He picked up one of the poles. They seemed solid enough.

The frame would need to be attached to the cabin; from there, the tarp could be suspended towards the front of the boat, with the ropes running back, attaching to the gunwales. That way, the boy could be at the wheel and easily get out to adjust the tarp.

That was the theory. Simple really. If he could make it work.

He looked up at the blades sweeping above his head and seemed to see, for the first time, the currents of air flowing through them.

He sat up on the jacket, using the edge of the platform to bend a panel from the engine housing. There was only enough rope to tie a strong knot at the main junction of the frame and then make the lines for adjusting the tarp, so he needed brackets for securing the frame to the cabin. He pushed down on the end of the panel, felt the metal reach the limit of its flex, then give just a few millimetres. He lifted it up and inspected the angle.

He'd gone down to the engine room earlier that day and dismantled what was left of the engine. He'd shifted the batteries and the heaviest components and secured them in a line running along the keel to rebalance the hull. He'd left the main workings in an old crate and taken only the housing panels and as many fastenings as he could find.

This was what it had come to – all those years learning how to fix the most technical mechanical problems and now all he needed were sheets of metal, nuts, bolts and screws. The number of times he had cleaned and serviced a drive shaft and now all it was good for was as a makeshift hammer for punching pilot holes in the walls of the cabin.

All those years his father spent trying to modify the engine, rigging up extra batteries, when it was engines and batteries that had kept him trapped.

He looked out towards the edge of the farm, then back at the turbines. The water was gurrelly and restless. Waves split off and ran in all directions, their edges dark and creased.

A wave rose up, slapped and peeled away from the base of the tower. He pushed down hard on the bracket and felt the metal give again.

He pulled on the rope and the tarp rose and fell. He shook the frame. It all seemed secure. It had taken days to get it right – attaching and reattaching the poles in different configurations to give it as much strength as possible, to make sure that the ropes would reach and the tarp had room to expand – but it was finally ready.

The boat was loaded with all of the supplies. He'd repaired the rain-collector and guttering system, removed the water filter from the coffee machine and rigged it up in the hold. He'd brought his roll-mat back down the tower and made up a bed in the cabin.

He tested the ropes one more time. The wind was blowing strong and clean from the west. If he cast off now, it would take him straight out of the farm. He went to the stern and looked out beyond the last rows. He had enough supplies. He could just uncouple the boat and be gone over the horizon. He would never see the farm again. He tried to imagine it – no turbines, no churning fields, just open water all around. No more failing systems, no more delayed supplies. No more tending to machines until they crumbled and broke for ever.

He had no idea what was out there. Even his father's map showed nothing beyond the mainland and the North Sea. But there were winds and there were currents and they all had to go somewhere.

He looked out again at the open sea. His hand gripped the rope. He felt each fibre against his skin.

The wind streamed out in front of him. He should go now. The currents were pushing in the right direction, there were hours of daylight left. He should probably have gone already.

The wind was so clean that he could feel each one of his hairs lifting slowly. He moved his hand slowly on the rope.

But he didn't cast off. Instead he looked back towards the cabin, at the gap where the battery gauge would have been, and tried to remember that night in the storm. He had forced himself not to think about it for so long that it had shrunk to something hard and dark in the back of his mind, like a knot in a piece of driftwood.

His chest tightened as he remembered again the waves, the sound of the wind, the old man's face as he'd gripped the strap. What if …? The boy shook his head. What were the chances, really, that the maintenance boat had survived intact, that its battery had held enough charge, that the old man had somehow been able to pilot it back to the rig? Almost none. He breathed out slowly. Almost none.

The old man would tell him to go. He would say that, now, the boy had no other option. He would say that there was nothing for him to go back for. He would say that if the boy went now, he would be piloting with the wind behind him, and that, if he got some stupid bloody notion in his head about going the other way, then he would be heading straight into the wind, which would be almost impossible. It could be weeks before it changed. And all that time he'd just have to wait, eating through his supplies, risking the return of another storm. Every day he waited he would be stacking the odds against himself. The old man would say that the boy would never have this chance again.

The boy tested the rope one more time. It was strong and flexible. The wind pushed against his back, making the surface of the water stream out towards the horizon.

He thought again about that late resupply and the bets the old man had made to let him win the tins. He thought about the cable the old man had cut, and how he would always find the boy the most intricate of jobs to occupy his time. How he would joke or bully or cajole whenever the boy was at his lowest. How he would force him to take a bet or play a game of pool or come out on some long detour through the fields to check his nets. How he had set off those flares that long winter, when the boy couldn't stand the gloom over the farm any more. How, for those first years, he'd made sure that the boy was so exhausted that he couldn't lie awake at night, couldn't dwell, couldn't think – always leaving him to decipher the maintenance report, setting him the most difficult repairs, making so much mess that the rig needed constant cleaning, making sure the boy was focused on the job, keeping him going.

How, when the boy had fallen in the dock, the old man had just told him to get up – get up now, he'd said – the urgency in his voice like sparks off a flint. He hadn't moved, hadn't reached down to help. Because if the boy hadn't got up then by himself, he probably never would.

On the deck there was a short length of rope that had been left over. The boy went across to it, picked it up and began to unwind its threads. It would make a serviceable fishing line, and he might as well do something while he waited for the wind to change.

The sky was dark but it had to be nearly morning. Out in the distance, a faint strip of light was becoming visible, as if a layer of paint was being slowly scratched away. The boy was sitting in one of the leather chairs, which he had brought down and bolted to the deck, just behind the wheel. He had even cut out a section of carpet to go under his roll-mat in the corner of the cabin.

He spent most of his time on the boat now, sleeping there overnight, sitting up all day in the lee of the tower. The weather could turn suddenly and he had to be ready.

The cabin was scattered with posters, the backs of which were covered in drawings and diagrams that the boy had made, showing the boat, the tarpaulin, the action of the wind. He'd raised and lowered the sheet, folded it away and unravelled it hundreds of times. He was sure he knew how it all worked, although he had never taken the boat out from the tower to test it. This close to the edge, he could too easily get swept out to the open sea.

There were times, though, when he thought he might have to go. When he woke to the same westerlies set in for another day, when he watched his supplies slowly diminishing. But he pushed the thoughts from his mind, settled back in his chair, cut some new hooks for his line.

He waited, and found ways to fill the days. He cleaned the boat, he checked the ropes, he tested the tarp, he sat up late into the night, drawing more diagrams on the backs of the posters. He ate only half a tin of food a day.

Sometimes, he thought he saw a band of different-coloured cloud drift across the horizon. Sometimes, he thought he saw the turbines far to the south shift their blades. There were days of heavy swell when the boat strained at its moorings, and days when the wind dropped and the blades barely completed a single circuit in an hour. Once, he had been up the tower and heard the yaw motors, then felt the nacelle begin to turn. He had rushed down the lift and out to the boat, but the turbine had just shifted a few degrees then gone back to its original position.

Gradually, the light increased, picking out the tips of the blades, then the rotor hubs, then the towers, until it seemed as though the turbines were floating. Down below, the sea was still dark. The boy got up and went to the stern to check his line. He had tied it to a spare pole so that it hung from a height and he could see it if it moved. He had even baited the hooks with some of the food from the tins, but there had been no sign of the fish since they'd drifted past. The water had stayed clear for one day and then settled back to its usual murk. The fish must have moved on. Either that or they couldn't stand the tinned food either.

The boy went back into the cabin, sat down in the chair, watched his line and waited.

It was moving. The line was moving, being drawn over to the right. The boy stood up, rubbed his eyes and stepped out of the cabin. He must have fallen asleep. Outside the deck was wet. When had it rained? He remembered a dream about a leak. He'd been having the same one again and again. He was pressing on a crack and water was pouring out, flooding the hull, and he was trying to block it with some rope and a rolled-up length of tarpaulin. Then someone had appeared, watching, but the boy always woke up at that exact moment, cold with sweat.

His line was moving. He took a few steps closer, then he realized the line wasn't moving – the line was staying still. It was the boat that was moving, being pushed by the changing current.

The mooring cables tightened, then the sliders began to shift and the boat slowly swung one hundred and eighty degrees to the opposite side of the tower. The boy stood on the deck and waited. The wind was still pushing from the west, lifting the swell into small peaks. The boat rocked and swung from side to side. The boy held on to the gunwale and looked up at the blades, sweeping the air far above him.

He watched and waited. The blades stayed facing west. Then, just as he felt his neck beginning to cramp, he heard a deep grating and the nacelle began to turn. The blades turned to face north, then north-east, then they finally settled facing out to the open sea.

The boy ran to the stern, pulled in his line, then went to the bow and took hold of the mooring cables. He had gone over and over exactly what he would do. He had drawn diagrams, worked out the angles, thought through every process. He looked back at the tarp, the bent framework of poles, the make-shift brackets and ancient ropes holding everything in place. What was he thinking? What the hell had he been thinking?

He felt instinctively in his pocket for his watch, then remembered it wasn't there. He looked up instead at the blades, which were all still facing east, beating steadily.

He took a deep breath, unhooked the mooring cables, pushed the boat out, ran to the ropes, unfurled the tarp, secured the lines, ran into the cabin, took hold of the wheel and waited.

Nothing happened.

The boat dipped in the swell, rolled from side to side and turned slowly. The boy held the wheel and waited. Nothing happened. He let go of the wheel and went out on deck. The tarp was just hanging, flapping in the wind. The boat rolled and turned. The boy pulled on the ropes, tightening and loosening the sheet. He took hold of the frame and shook it. The boat turned. Then suddenly the ropes pulled tight, the tarp snapped and bulged, the boat lurched forward and the deck tilted violently to port. The boy stumbled, heard the frame creak loudly. The deck continued to tilt. The boat picked up speed. The boy staggered into the cabin, took hold of the wheel and tried to turn it to starboard.

He stood in the tilting cabin, wrestling with the wheel. Eventually he got the boat almost level and looked up just in time to see a turbine looming straight ahead. He let go of the wheel and the boat swung away. The deck lurched. The starboard window rose, giving a view of the full height of the tower as the boat veered past.

The boy gripped the wheel and pulled at it again, inching the rudder against the pressure of the water. Slowly, the boat righted, then seemed to twist, suddenly, the other way. The stern swung round so the bow was facing into the wind and, as quickly as it had filled, the tarp went slack.

The boy stood, gripping the wheel, breathing heavily. There was no sign of the turbine he'd come from. There was no sign of the edge of the farm. He had almost capsized and crashed, and it turned out he had no idea how his boat worked. But it had worked.

He held the wheel and waited. Slowly, the boat began to turn again.

c.9,500 Before Present

A boat floats above a valley, above grassland and heathland, above the stumps of long-dead trees.

The valley blooms with mussels, clams and whelks. The water is clear and still. Birds dive down to pluck weed from among the branches and lever up spongy crusts of wood. The old rivers are now trenches on the seabed – filling with silt until they're barely visible, like old pathways where no one walks any more.

The boat moves on, making for a wide estuary, following a route where, during the last spring tide, a new channel was formed.

The trees were the first to go, oak and lime drowning in the rising water table, even when the coastline was still out of sight. It was a slow and quiet way to disappear. It was painless, relatively. The ground became sodden. Bogs appeared, and marshes.

Water pooled in hollows and became lakes. Rivers widened and linked hands. Almost overnight, grassland sprouted to reed. At the next full moon, the reeds were swallowed by the tide.

Down in the marsh there's a shelter of reeds, built on a raft of reeds. The boat noses in. The raft creaks and presses lower in the water.

There is no wood any more, barely enough dry brush to start a fire. Salt has worked its way into the soil, choking the roots of everything but samphire and cord grass. There is a constant, brackish damp. When the wind drops, the air is thick with flies.

The hut fills with smoke. Inside, in blackened baskets, are the bones of animals, carved into the forms of animals that haven't been seen in living memory.

Hunters burned the last of the thickets to drive them out into the open. Now the hunters are driven out. It's a slow and quiet way to disappear. It is painless, relatively. The only people left are those who can endure the damp and the cold and the flies; those who have a taste for raw shellfish and the reeking flesh of seabirds.

The boat rises on the incoming tide. It strains at its moorings. The tide comes in and doesn't drop out. Next year there will be less land, more flies. Next year, the shelter will be gone.

Easterlies

He thought he knew the wind before – the way it worked, the way it moved, its quirks and temperaments – but without the mediation of gearbox or blade control, it was sprawling and volatile. Looking up at the turbines, it seemed like the wind was blowing cleanly, but down on the surface, gusts cut in every direction, causing the tarp to flap and buckle, and the boat to be dragged suddenly off-course, veering between the rows.

Sometimes the wind would squall for days – the tiller would drag, the tarp would never be at the right tension. The boy would rush from wheel to ropes to wheel. He would have to climb on top of the cabin and free a tangled corner. Sometimes he would be making good progress, then one of the brackets on the frame would loosen and he would have to furl the tarp and make a hasty repair. By the time he'd finished and was ready to go, the wind would have dropped.

He'd been prepared for the difficulties of using the tarp, the difficulties of navigation, but he hadn't been prepared for the physical toll. All those weeks shut up in the nacelle had sapped his strength; he had no stamina, his limbs were sluggish, his joints weak. Some days it would be so exhausting simply getting the tarp to the right tension – constantly running back and forth to adjust the ropes – that the wind would change and he wouldn't have the energy to do anything about it. The boat would drift back the entire distance it had already travelled before he could get up the strength to haul in the tarp and think about mooring up.

He would travel each day for as long as the wind held or he could stay on his feet, then he would pick a turbine where he would spend the night. He became adept at piloting the boat in, casting the tow-line and lowering the tarp at exactly the right moment to bring the boat to a steady stop. Apart from once or twice, when he miscalculated and had to fend off the fast-approaching jacket with a pole. Apart from once or twice, when a horrible crunch emanated from the bow.

The first thing he would always do after he moored up was take the lift to the top of the turbine. But he never found another one with a table and chairs in the room at the back. He never found another coffee machine. So he would go out and spend the night on the boat. He would sit in the chair, wrapped in a sheet, eat a little food, drink a little water and lower his fishing line from the stern. All he ever caught was junk – bits of rubber tubing, fragments of old gleaming packets – but still he would sit out until the last light, watching his line, trying not to think about what he would find back at the rig, if he ever got back to the rig; thinking instead about that huge shoal, wondering where they were.

Gradually his body became more used to the work – his back ached less and his hands grew thick calluses against the chafing of the ropes. Each day he was able to keep going a little longer. Sometimes, if the wind was right, he would sail through the night. With no engine noise, he could listen for the sound of the water breaking against the towers and guide the boat that way. Sometimes, there would be a glimmer of light in the sky. Sometimes, the clouds would open up, revealing a hole dusted with bright flecks.

If the weather turned, he would have to moor up and wait it out. There were times when sudden gales blew in and it took twenty or thirty passes before he could hook onto a jacket. There were times when the sea rose up and it was too dangerous to get close to the towers, so he would manoeuvre the boat to the open water between the fields, lower the tarp and ride it out. There were times when there was nothing he could do to stop himself being blown back miles the way he'd come.

But he learned how to sail across the wind, and he worked out that if he travelled in a zigzag route, he could actually make headway running against it. To begin with, he would navigate by the corrosion on the towers, but gradually he learned the different ways the currents moved throughout the farm. Those from the south were weaker, easy enough to travel against; those from the north brought big swells that broke across the bow. It was better to just let them take the boat, then cut back when they slackened.

Sometimes the boat would seem to skim along the surface of the water; other times progress would be laboured and sluggish. Most days he tried not to think about whether he'd ever get back. He tried not to think of the size of the farm, the vast identical rows. What he thought of was the tension of the ropes, the angle of the wheel, how long a steady breeze would last.

One day he passed a turbine with a scorch mark halfway up its tower. He turned and watched it as he went past. He'd already passed that turbine a few days before. He remembered the dark, peeling paint – the way it curled off into the wind like flags. A few days later he passed it again. He began to see it every few days – he almost started looking out for it just before it came into view. However hard he tried to change his route, however much he tacked further north, further west, he always circled back to the turbine with the scorched paint.

One time he was sure he smelled the burnt veneer on the wind before he got there. Another time he got so close he could see the blisters rupturing the grey skin.

His eyes stung with wind and salt. He couldn't remember what the open sea had looked like.

Days passed, then weeks, maybe months. Finally, the turbines got smaller and the fields seemed more familiar. Then one evening he moored up to a tower and, when he went up into the nacelle, he found a repair. He studied it for a long time, trying to work out if it was one of his.

Mainly he kept heading west, but sometimes he would see a row that he thought he recognized, or a particular transformer, and he would turn off to the north or south and follow some half-remembered route until night came, or he realized that he actually didn't remember it at all.

Then, one day, he looked down a row and saw, at the end of it, the squat outline of the rig.

The dock gates were open and inside was dark. The boy took a deep breath and brought the boat round as slowly as he could, peering forward into the gloom. When he was nearing the gates, he locked the wheel, went out on deck and lowered the tarp. The boat slowed. Then he picked up a pole, stood in the bow and guided the boat in.

Inside, the dock was quiet. His eyes refocused just in time to fend off the walkway and bring the boat in to a steady stop. He stood in the bow and looked around. The storm had wrecked the dock. The walkway was buckled and several panels were missing. The crates that had been stacked to the side had been bowled into the water. There was a layer of rubbish floating in one corner. Two of the strip lights were hanging from their wires and the other two had been torn completely loose.

There was no sign of the maintenance boat.

The boy stood there for a long time. He watched a piece of netting drift and then sink into the murk. The storm waves crashed in his head, the cabin door swung open and shut and open again. Then he stepped down over the gunwale, attached the mooring cables and made his way up into the rig. The lights in the stairwell flickered. There was a tide-line of scum and plastic fragments on the stairs, where the water must have reached during the storm's peak.

The corridors were dank and cold. There was no sound coming from the air vents. The computers in the control room had powered down. Only their blinking standby lights showed that they were still working.

In the rec room, the buckled legs of the pool table had finally given way and it was slumped on its side, balls scattered across the floor. The window had a large crack running from top to bottom.

An awful smell hung in the galley, emanating from a tin of something left open and rotting on the side. The boy picked it up and put it in the rubbish chute, then got a mug and poured himself a drink of water. The other mug was standing next to the sink, stuck to the counter by a hardened ring of homebrew.

The boy went down to the sleeping quarters and opened the door to his room. There was the bed, the built-in furniture and the small stack of technical manuals on the floor. Had it always been this empty? He had spent so many weeks on the cramped boat that his room suddenly felt bare and anonymous. He went back out and shut the door.

Further up the corridor a ventilation pipe was dripping. He stood and listened and the drip grew louder, until it was pounding in his skull, causing his ears to ring. He walked over, grabbed hold of the pipe and pushed it upwards. The pipe creaked and its ceiling mounts buckled. The veins stood out on the boy's arms. The pipe bent and split along the top. The boy gripped it harder until his hands went white. He pushed until it wouldn't move any more, then he let his arms drop to his sides and stood, shaking. The dripping stopped.

The boy closed his eyes, took a deep breath and then another. Finally, he made himself go over to the old man's room. He stood outside it for a long time. If he didn't go in there, if he didn't open the door, he could imagine the old man was inside. He could almost hear him, checking through his nets, talking to himself, humming. He opened the door.

The room was the same as he'd last seen it – the maps of the farm, the piles of netting, the containers of mud and sand on every surface, the same smell of homebrew, which was fainter now, barely more than a trace, lingering in the corners like dust.

The boy stood in the doorway, running his eyes over everything. Then he crossed the room, moved the maps out of the way and sat down on the bed.

The whole room seemed to pitch and roll. He told himself it was just his body playing tricks – still compensating for the movement of the boat. His left leg tensed, and then his right. He concentrated and tried to make them stop. The walls rose and fell. It was just muscle memory; he could make them stop. He sat very still on the bed. The room shifted around him.

He closed his eyes. Salt stung the backs of his eyelids. He had to think. He had to make a plan. Supplies – that's what he needed. Supplies and spare water filters. His tools. He needed to fix up the boat and then go.

One by one, he began to go through all of the repairs he needed to do to the boat. He went through the processes, the exact tools he would use. The bed seemed to slide beneath him. He reached out a hand to brace himself and touched against something metal. He opened his eyes, saw the striped deck-chair, the tattered blanket thrown across it. The floor lurched. His stomach lurched and he thought he was about to be sick.

There was a loud crash.

The boy jumped up, stumbled, steadied himself and listened. There was silence, then a series of quieter noises coming from further down in the rig. He left the room and walked down the stairs. As he got closer, he heard movement in the dock. When he looked through the hatchway everything was dark. The gates were still open, but beyond it was night. The light from the hatchway cast a bright rectangle and, further up along the gangway, a torch flickered, picking out the hull of the boy's boat and the shape of another vessel moored up next to it.

Suddenly, the beam stopped and swung round to the hatchway. 'Who's there,' said the boy and another voice at exactly the same time.

The boy stepped forward, and the torch moved closer along the gangway, focusing in on the boy's face. He blinked, raised his hand.

'Move your hand.' The voice was loud, but its sharp edges seemed to get smothered in the dark.

The boy lowered his hand and squinted into the light.

The light stayed focused on his face for a long time, then the torch clicked off and the old man appeared from the gloom. His hair had grown long and straggly. It was still black, but his face was blurred with a ragged grey beard. He had red rims around his eyes and he kept twitching his jaw. He was still pointing the torch at the boy with one hand. The other gripped a pry bar.

The boy didn't move. Then he reached up, rubbed the side of his jaw, and realized that he too had a beard and matted hair down over his ears.

'That your boat?' the old man said.

The boy nodded.

'You can't leave it there.'

The boy nodded again and stepped back to let the old man past.

Halfway up the stairs the old man stopped. 'So you're back then,' he said.

'I'm back.'

The old man nodded, turned off to the sleeping quarters, went into his room and closed the door.

The boy showered, shaved and cut his hair. The clippers jammed and stopped working, so he had to settle for hacking away lumps of salt-stiff hair with a pair of blunt scissors, tidying it up as best he could. In the galley he found that the crates stacked in the corner were all full of tins. There must have been a resupply in the time he was away. He wondered, for a moment, whether the pilot would have noticed his absence, what the old man would have said. He supposed the old man must have said nothing, otherwise they'd have sent someone else out to take his place.

He went to the cupboard and found a tin of protein mince, then took four sachets of flavouring from the other tins.

Once he'd eaten, he sat for some time, savouring the feeling of hot food in his stomach. Then he went to his room and lay on the bed. The mattress rocked and steadied. The bed was still. The walls were still. The wind and the waves felt a long way off. He closed his eyes, then opened them, got up and went down to spend the night on the boat.

He had almost forgotten the sounds of the rig – the hum of the electrics, the cooling system, how the metal creaked, how the water thumped and thrummed through the supports.

The boy sat up. The dock was dark, but he could hear footsteps and rattling breath. Then a torch switched on, lighting up the old man's hands and feet where he was crouching at the other end of the gangway. He had a bundle of netting, which he lowered down and then dragged through the water.

The boy looked out of the cabin window and watched. The old man stayed crouching on the edge of the gangway, dragging his net back and forth. After a while he pulled his net in and then began to shake it into a bucket. The boy didn't see anything fall out of the net, but eventually the old man stopped, picked up the bucket and made his way back up into the rig. The boy waited for a moment, then left the cabin and followed.

The door to the old man's room was open and the light was on inside. The boy stayed in the corridor and listened, but heard nothing so he walked over and stepped into the room.

The old man was sitting in his deckchair with the bucket on his lap. He reached in with a tiny sieve and began scooping out what looked like grains of sand, spreading them out on top of the chest of drawers. He leaned down, his face only a few inches from the surface, and began sorting the grains into different piles with the tip of a knife.

The boy took another step. As the piles grew, he could see that they were all different colours. He looked into the containers nearest to him. One's contents were blue; another's were bright green. Blue and green sand? He looked closer. They weren't sand. All of the containers in the room were full of tiny fragments of plastic, sorted and stored according to colour and size.

Now he looked again, the nets piled up around the room were not the same thick nets that had been there before. They were fine meshes and gauzes, what looked like filters taken from the water system and the air vents, all choked with minute pieces of plastic.

'Where did you find it all?' the boy said.

The old man didn't look up. 'Find it?' he said eventually. 'I didn't find it. It's just there. In the water.' He stifled a cough. 'I saw it when I was looking. I looked and looked.' He went back to sorting through the grains. 'I didn't find anything.'

The boy was about to speak, then he noticed that all of the maps scattered across the bed were of the eastern fields. The old man had marked in the open area of water where they had been caught by the storm. Along the sides of the maps he had scribbled numbers and calculations – wind-speed measurements, the direction of the currents. Each individual turbine all around the place where the boy had been swept away was marked with a cross. The old man had crossed off all of the turbines in the eastern half of zone three and those for almost twenty miles into the outer fields.

On the bedside unit, among more tins and scraps of paper, was the boy's fishing line. The boy picked it up.

'You hadn't caught anything,' the old man said, without looking up.

'I'll get us out of here,' the boy said.

The old man pushed a tiny piece of plastic over to the far side of the surface.

'We can leave in a few days. As soon as I've fixed up the boat. We don't need to wait for anything. That boat – it can go anywhere. It doesn't need batteries. It …'

One of the pieces caught on the tip of the knife and flicked onto the floor. The old man got down off his chair and began feeling around in the piles of netting. He picked up a net and shook it out, scattering more plastic across the room. He pressed his hand against the floor and, when he lifted it up, it was covered in multicoloured fragments. He stayed kneeling on the floor, staring at his hand.

The boy waited until he realized that the old man wasn't going to get back up, then he left the room and closed the door. As he walked down the corridor he heard the old man searching through his nets, muttering to himself, his voice low and grating. Then there was the familiar catch, the rattling breath and the old man began to cough.

Cracks

The boy woke slumped against the corridor wall, his neck bent at a painful angle. He had stayed outside the old man's room all night, waiting for the coughing to stop, which it must have done, because the room was now quiet. He straightened his neck slowly and pulled himself to his feet. He went to the old man's door and listened for a moment, then carried on down the corridor.

The first thing he did was reboot the computer and get the air con working again. The vents rattled back to life and slowly began to shift the rig's stale air. Then he made his way down to the dock and began to clear a space so he could get to work on his boat.

He scooped out the rubbish that was floating in the water and gathered together the tangled debris left over from the storm. He packed it all in the maintenance boat, then piloted out past the gates and dumped it in the sea. Then he piloted back, took his toolbag out of the hold and set to work repairing the dock.

Soon he'd patched the gangway and got both strip lights working. He took his time, enjoying the feeling of having his old tools in his hands. Then he fixed extra LED spots around the charging bay and hoisted his boat up to inspect the hull.

It was covered in scrapes and dents and there was a crack running down the bow, where he'd come in at a turbine too fast. He ran his hand over it. It had spread down until it was almost at the waterline. A few more weeks and that would have made the journey interesting.

He looked up at the threadbare tarp. Every edge was fraying. The frame creaked, looked like it would buckle at any minute. He picked up his welding torch, feeling its reassuring weight. The flame cast a small circle of light.

Once he'd fixed the crack, he scoured down the hull and gave it a new coat of rustproof paint. While that dried, he went up on deck to see what could be done about the framework for the tarp.

He removed all of the old, tattered ropes and dismantled the loose fixings. Some of the poles were bent out of shape, and those that could not be straightened were discarded. He had been thinking about a new structure for the frame, based around a central pole with a crossbeam. That would give him more manoeuvrability and allow the whole thing to be taken down in stormy weather. He rigged up a series of pulleys that fed the ropes into the cabin, so the tarp could be adjusted without leaving the wheel. He'd been able to manage the boat on his own, just, but with a crew of two it would be easy.

He was still working when the light outside grew faint and darkness began to spread in through the open gates. He'd been down at the boat all day; had not even stopped to eat. The wind pushed in and swirled round the dock. It would be steady all night and into the following day. He could feel the way the boat would respond to it, the way it would move over the surface of the sea.

The supplies in the galley would last him and the old man months on the boat. If he could find a way to rig up a battery, they might even be able to take the microwave with them. He emptied a tin of protein mince into a bowl and mashed it down with a fork. He wished he could get a cup of coffee. He reached into the cupboard and took down a jar of powdered tea, sniffed it and put it away again. He wondered if the old man had ever drunk real coffee. He should ask him.

The old man's mug was in the same place it had been the night before and there was no sign that any other plates or bowls had been used. The boy put his food in the microwave, set the timer and went back out into the corridor.

The rec room and control room were empty. When he got down to the sleeping quarters, he found the door to the old man's room still shut. He went up to it and knocked lightly. There was no answer. He pressed his ear to the metal, but could hear nothing. He knocked louder, waited, then opened the door.

The deckchair had tipped over and the old man was lying on the floor. The boy was there in a second. He knelt down, hesitated for a moment, then reached out and placed his hand on the old man's shoulder. The old man didn't stir. The boy stayed still, watching for any sign of movement. A small patch of condensation grew and receded on the floor next to the old man's mouth.

He got up, pushed the boxes and maps off the bed, then stooped down and picked the old man up. It was a shock how easy it was. The old man's hips and shoulder blades were sharp through his overalls. The boy laid him carefully on the bed, then ran from the room and came back with a mug of water.

He knelt down by the side of the bed, lifted the old man's head and held the mug to his mouth. The old man's lips were cracked. The skin on the back of his neck was hot and almost papery. The tendons at the base of his skull tensed beneath his matted hair as he tried to swallow. His throat gurgled and most of the water trickled down his beard.

The boy stayed kneeling by the bed. The old man's breath was shallow and rasping, his jaw slack. The air con whined and pushed dust around the room. One of the maps on the floor kept catching in the breeze – its corner rising and falling. The boy watched the old man's chest barely rise and fall. He just needed to wait. The old man would get better. He always got better. Any moment now, he'd open his eyes and ask what the hell the boy was doing in his room.

The boy knelt in silence. He should say something. That was what you did at times like this – you said something. The corner of the map rose and fell.

'It's a simple system,' the boy said. 'It uses the wind. You pull on these ropes and they open the tarp. Then the wind hits it and pushes the boat along. You adjust the tension by …'

'Sails,' said the old man, his voice barely audible.

The boy leaned in closer. 'What?'

'The tarp. It's called a sail.' He swallowed gratingly. 'The ropes are rigging.'

The boy nodded. 'Sails … rigging.'

'Jem.'

The boy looked down at the old man.

'You're back.'

The boy sat in the rec room with all of their medical supplies spread out across the low table in front of him. There were two rolls of yellowing bandages, two bottles of painkillers, a few blisters of sickness pills and a single, buckled tube of anaesthetic cream, which had crystallized and turned a strange pink colour. The wind made a high-pitched buzzing as it forced its way in through the crack in the window. Outside, beyond the scratched glass, a turbine shuddered to a halt. The boy stared out at the turbine, and then down at the supplies.

He'd stayed with the old man all night. There were times when it seemed that the old man was asleep, then the boy would see his eyes open, staring at the ceiling. At some point the coughing started and there was nothing the boy could do to stop it. He just had to sit and watch, and place his hand on the old man's shoulder and feel his frame shudder with each breath.

As he'd waited and watched the old man, he'd started to see old scars and injuries that he hadn't really noticed before. He didn't know when or how the old man had got most of them, but some he remembered: the burn on his forearm, which he'd got when he'd been welding with a mug of homebrew too close to his elbow. A bruise on his neck that had never fully healed, from a falling panel. A split thumbnail, the swollen bone in his ankle that clicked and locked and meant that sometimes he had to walk downstairs backwards. There was that weird dent in his forehead and a scar that he'd got when the boy had dropped that grinding disc, layered over it, like the maps of the seabed, or the maps of the coastline which showed how the land had changed and eroded.

In the morning, the boy had managed to get him to eat a little, drink a few sips of water, but every time the old man swallowed, it was accompanied by a grimace. His eyes roved across the ceiling. His skin, instead of burning, was now cold as the metal doorways. The boy had tried to give him one of the painkillers, but the damp must have got into the bottle, because when he poured out the tablets they turned into a grainy paste on his palm.

The boy leaned back and closed his eyes. He slept for maybe thirty seconds, then jerked awake, his heart hammering. The technical manuals said that when a piece of machinery was failing the mechanic needed to pay attention, to stay focused. They said that the mechanic should consider every viable solution before declaring the apparatus beyond repair. There was an image of a broken engine, its components laid out cold and still on the page.

He reached over and picked up the tube of cream. The thin metal had split where it had been bent and twisted, and the foiled lettering came off in dark specks that stuck to his fingers. He dropped it back down on the table.

The old man barely moved, apart from his hands, which clutched at the sheets, and his jaw, which twitched, tensed and went slack, as though an electrical current was passing through it.

The boy stood in the middle of the old man's room. He watched the old man's hands and jaw, he breathed slowly, he clenched and unclenched his own hands, looked around at the bottles and nets and fragments of plastic covering the floor. He bent down, picked up one of the nets and folded it carefully over his arm.

He picked up all of the nets, took them into the corridor, shook them out, folded them and stacked them in one of the empty rooms. Then he cleaned the floor, working square by square, mopping and drying each one in turn, scrubbing away at the decades of mud and salt and who knew what else.

He took the bottles of plastic grains and lined them up on top of the wardrobe and chest of drawers. He tried to arrange them by colour for the old man, but many of them were so similar that it was hard to tell them apart. He held one up and turned it in the light. Were the bits of plastic blue or green?

Sometimes they looked blue, sometimes green. Or maybe they were a mixture, a slow graduation from one colour to the other. He stared at the bottles harder.

'What are you doing?' the old man said, his voice faint and rasping.

The boy blinked, then looked round at the old man. 'We need to get you medicine,' he said.

The old man turned his head slightly to face the wall. 'I'm fine.'

'We can't leave until you're better.'

'Just need to get up.' The old man pushed himself onto his elbows and tried to lever himself up. His arms shook, he screwed his eyes shut and bit down, then finally let himself slump back onto the bed. He lay, breathing heavily. 'Why are you still here?' he said, almost too quietly to hear.

'What?'

The old man stared up at the ceiling. Then closed his eyes.

The boy reached over to one of the bottles on the chest of drawers and shifted it a few millimetres so it was in line with the others. 'You need medicine.'

The old man kept his eyes shut.

'There's only one way to get it.' The boy looked down at his hands. All he could hear was the way the old man was breathing. 'Last time I saw him, he told me what he wanted.'

The old man's eyes opened. They were bloodshot round the edges, and the skin underneath looked raw.

The boy stayed looking at his hands. 'The stuff you had in this room. I need it. *We* need it.'

The old man didn't move. He coughed, once, but managed to stop it before it turned into anything more. The room was too warm, too quiet. 'It's gone,' he said.

The boy looked up. He could suddenly smell the bleach he'd been using. It went up his nose, into his eyes and throat. He took a step closer to the bed. 'We need it. It's the only thing he wants.'

The old man said nothing. He closed his eyes and turned over to face the wall.

The boy sat in the cabin of his boat, where it was moored in the still waters of the dock. He sat cross-legged on the floor and traced the scratches embedded in there: countless pacings of boots – his own, his father's – countless nicks from where he'd skidded across in rough weather, and his chair had fallen over, and he'd ended up sleeping crouched down on his front, his head tucked into his arms, his nails digging in to try to stop the constant pitching.

He pulled on one of the ropes and the tarp unfurled. The fabric didn't even stir in the dock's still air. The wind thumped against the outer walls. He folded the tarp up again carefully.

The old man was getting worse. He'd tried telling himself that this wasn't true – that every time the old man drank some water, or ate a little food, he was getting better – but he couldn't tell himself that any more.

He'd counted the tins in the galley and tried to work out how long it had been since the pilot's last visit, and when he

212

might be expected to return. But it was impossible to say. The old man had hardly been eating and neither had the boy. The days blurred into one another in the old man's hot, cramped room.

When the old man was asleep, the boy would take the maintenance boat out and scour the turbines for any sign of the old man's stuff. But he didn't dare stay away for longer than a few hours and soon he had searched every turbine within that radius.

He stared at the maps in the old man's room for hours, searching for any clue, but found nothing. So he resorted to talking – trying to convince the old man to say where he had hidden it, trying to keep the frustration and panic out of his voice and only sometimes succeeding. But as the old man grew weaker, his speech became strained, his thoughts more and more disjointed. Sometimes he wouldn't seem to notice that the boy was there; other times he would grip the boy's hand and stare straight at him.

'Where is it?' the boy would ask. 'Where is it?'

But all the old man would say was, 'It's gone.'

c.8,500 Before Present

There is nothing but sand now, and the wind. And each day the wind scours more grains into the sea.

The island sits low in the water, barely troubling the horizon. With each storm, its outline shifts.

Sometimes the drifting sand reveals a trace of something – a midden of shells, a sharpened stone, a pile of crushed thatch – but as soon as it's unearthed, it's covered over again.

The sand is a maze of seabirds' burrows. The tunnels are long and dark and hollow. On still nights there is no sound except for the waves, and the murmuring of the birds deep in the dunes. Before dawn they leave, rushing silently out to sea.

*

Across the sea, on distant coastlines, people stand on beaches, looking out towards the island. Some days they can see it above the waves, most days they can't. On clear nights they see the birds rise up, like grains of sand, or a spirit leaving a body.

Sometimes, on their own tide-line, ghosts appear – masses of blackened roots, clods of peat, petrified stumps preserved in bell jars of salt. They leave offerings. They float out the bodies of the dead.

They tell stories of ancestors who walked in forests on the seabed, of the island that was once a coastline, a coastline that was once a range of hills at the heart of a continent, a continent that was once frozen and covered over by ice.

Nothing

The supply boat turned a slow arc and backed in. The fenders thumped against the dock, where the boy stood, alone, next to four crates of turbine parts, cleaned and neatly packed. There was no movement for a long time. Then, finally, the cabin door opened and the pilot appeared at the stern. He paused, looked the boy up and down, then scanned across to the charging bay, where the maintenance boat was hoisted up.

When the boy had seen the supply boat appear on the map, he had towed his boat out and hidden it in the fields. Then he'd packed away his tools in the storeroom, cleaned the charging bay of any traces of paint or solder. The dock was as it had always looked.

The pilot blinked, nodded, threw the boy the ropes and watched carefully as the knots were tied. The boy passed up the charging cable. The pilot blinked again, turned and plugged the cable into the socket. 'If you'd care to examine the goods,' he said, lowering the gangplank down to where the boy was standing.

The pilot leaned against a crate and folded his hands over his stomach. The light coming down into the hold fell in strips across his body, highlighting only his belt, his shoulders, the top half of his face. 'Medicine?' He furrowed his brow and his eyes disappeared. 'Medicine's very expensive.'

'I've got any parts you need.' The boy gestured to the crates he'd carried on board. 'Generators, gearboxes.' He forced himself to sit down, even though he wanted to pace, to shove the crates at the pilot and make him look inside. He leaned back and put his hands in his pockets.

The pilot sighed. 'It's not that I don't want to help. It's just that the situation is … difficult.'

'So difficult people don't need working generators?'

The pilot's face shifted into what might have been a smile. 'Oh no. I'm sure they need them. But you see, therein lies my predicament.'

The boy glanced across at the crates. It had taken him weeks to find enough working parts. Days to clean and test them. He'd shut down every decent turbine in a ten-mile radius of the rig. At night he could hardly hear any blades thrumming; he'd jolted awake once and not known where he was.

'What predicament?' he said eventually.

'I'm glad you asked,' the pilot said. 'It's good to know that there are some people who still have consideration for the feelings of others.' He adjusted his position on the crate. 'You know, it's a long trip out here. Thirsty work. I don't suppose …'

'We're all out.'

'A shame.' The pilot clasped his hands and rolled his thumbs, one on top of the other. His fingernails caught a narrow band of light. 'I do find it difficult to express my full meaning when I'm thirsty.'

The boy breathed out heavily and got up. 'Wait here.'

'True consideration,' the pilot called after him. 'True hospitality.'

The boy found an unopened bottle of homebrew tucked behind the disused distillery. From the colour of it, it looked like it could have been from the old man's experimental phase. The boy had once found him prying the letters off one of the rig's warning signs and scattering them into the vats. He said the brew needed more character.

Now the pipes and containers were coated in greasy dust. Nothing glugged or bubbled; the containers were cold and empty. He wiped the dust off the bottle with his sleeve, picked up a mug from the galley and went back down to the dock.

When he returned he found the pilot sitting in a fold-out chair with an upturned crate in front of him. There was no sign that he had even looked at the turbine parts.

The boy put the bottle and mug on the crate.

The pilot sat back, looked from the boy to the bottle, to the mug and back again.

The boy clenched his fist in his pocket, then picked up the bottle and poured the pilot a drink.

'Now, we were discussing need.' The pilot picked up his mug. 'One would assume it would be a simple matter. You need something and I give it to you.' He took a sip, flinched. 'Very full-bodied,' he said.

The boy waited. A drop of homebrew slid slowly down the side of the bottle. He watched it reach the bottom and then pool on the top of the crate. He knew he shouldn't ask – the pilot wanted him to ask and he shouldn't do it. He watched another drop slowly start to slide. 'So will you?' he said.

'Will I what?'

'Give me what I need?'

'Oh.' The pilot blinked, looked down into his mug. 'Well, of course I would but, you see, my predicament.' He raised his mug to his mouth, then lowered it again. 'If I were to give everyone everything they needed, where would that leave me?' He looked up at the boy.

The boy looked down at him.

'Not here.' The pilot leaned forward and tapped on the crate. 'Certainly not here, arranging trades.' The bottle rocked and he frowned, reached out and steadied it. 'Because if I gave everyone everything they needed, there'd be no *need* to trade any more, would there?'

The boy stepped forward. 'Look, I just need …'

'No, no, no, no, no.' The pilot got up, walked to the other side of the hold and looked out of the porthole. 'This won't do. *Need* doesn't get us anywhere. I can't trade with people who *need* things. It's far too …' he put his mug down on a crate next to him and wiped his hands lightly on his stomach '… it's far too messy.'

The boy stayed where he was. The smell of the homebrew rose up into the small room, until he could almost taste it in the back of his throat. It smelled like the winter batch when the old man had de-iced the pipes and then forgotten to clean them out again. 'So what do you want me to say?'

'Want.' The pilot turned round and raised a finger. 'Now we're getting somewhere. *Want* is something I can work with.' He picked up his mug again, took a sip, studied the liquid for a long while and then nodded. 'One should always trade for something one *wants*. Keeps it businesslike. Keeps it so there's no hard feelings.'

The boy thought of the old man. He seemed to have stabilized in recent days, but the night before, he had been coughing again for hours. When the boy had left him that morning his breath had been thin and shallow. The boy had had to lean in so close to check on the old man that he'd felt the dryness of it against his face.

'So, what do you want?' he said slowly and evenly.

The pilot took a long drink, walked over to the bottle and filled his mug to the brim. 'That,' he said, 'is a far more reasonable question.'

'I'll get you his stuff,' the boy said. 'I just need time. When he gets better, he'll tell me where it is, then …'

'That doesn't matter.'

'I'll get it.'

'You misunderstand.' The pilot put down his mug, went

to the back of the hold and returned with a crate, which he dropped at the boy's feet.

The boy opened the lid. Inside were bones, blades, carved stones, polished wood – the best of all the things the old man had trawled up over the years. They looked so small, barely filling half the crate, so neatly cleaned and polished, packaged carefully in rows.

'I'm afraid,' the pilot said, picking up his mug again, 'there's no market for any of it.'

The boy looked down at the objects in the crate. There was the piece of twisted wood that looked like a flame, and the clutch of green stones, and the tooth the size of the boy's clenched fist, which he used to pick up and stare at, unable to believe that it had once belonged to something that had lived.

And there were other things he'd never seen before. There was a pointed piece of bone that looked like a turbine blade, and a dark stone in the shape of a boat, which the old man had wrapped neatly in paper.

One of the green stones was chipped. The boy didn't think it had been chipped before. He reached down and picked it up. There was a small line in one corner of the smooth, green edge. He ran his finger along it, trying to polish it away, but the chip stayed where it was.

The pilot sat back down in his fold-out chair. The springs grated quietly. 'I was surprised too. He had it all ready when I arrived last time. Said he wanted to trade for a new battery.'

The boy stepped back from the crate, leaned against the wall of the hold and closed his eyes. He suddenly felt very tired.

'It was an easier trade than I was expecting. He gave up the whole lot right away.' The pilot paused. There was the sound of his lips against the tin mug, the gurgle of his throat. 'But then, you see, he said he *needed* to get to the outer fields.'

The boy still had his eyes shut, but he could tell the pilot was watching him closely.

'He didn't tell me what had happened right away. First of all he said you were just out making repairs. But I knew. The way he was acting. It was just like last time.'

The boy opened his eyes. The pilot was looking right at him.

'You know, he was out here on his own for over a year before he let me report your father. Kept telling me he was just out working. That he always just happened to be out working whenever I turned up. I thought I was going to have to go through that whole rigmarole again. The statements, the reports, all that paperwork.' His nose and mouth pinched together again. 'So it really is fortunate to see you alive and well.'

The pilot leaned over to the crate of the old man's stuff, took out a polished, lumpy pebble and held it to the light. 'What do you suppose this was for?'

The boy stepped forward, his heart hammering in his throat. His fists were clenched again but this time he didn't try to hide them in his pockets. 'What do you want?'

The pilot turned the pebble in the light, stopped, frowned, dropped it back in the crate and wiped his hand on his overalls. 'Thank God for civilization.'

The boy stepped forward again and closed the crate with a bang. 'What do you—'

'I want to see him.'

'What?'

'I want to see him.'

'No.'

The pilot put down his mug and folded his arms. 'Well then, I can't help.' He breathed out slowly through his nose. 'You want medicine. Well, assuming that we can come to an agreement on the price, I will have to make sure that I procure the correct drugs. And for that I will have to see him.'

The boy stood still for a long time, then he turned towards the hatch.

The boat rocked gently as they made their way across the deck.

'So he just found you?' the pilot said.

'What?'

'The old man, he just found you?'

The boy reached up and rubbed his jaw. 'He just found me.'

'In the outer fields?'

The boy nodded.

'Washed up on a turbine?' The pilot stopped and looked over at the maintenance boat suspended in the charging bay. 'All that in a boat without a decent battery.'

The boy watched the side of the pilot's face as it turned, scanning the dock. The lines around the pilot's eyes were small and fine and neatly spaced.

'Amazing,' the pilot said eventually.

There was a noise from down below the gunwale. 'It is, isn't it. But then sometimes I surprise even myself.'

They looked down and saw the old man standing at the bottom of the gangplank. He had slicked his hair back and was wearing clean overalls. It looked like he had his hand resting on the railing next to him, but the boy could tell he was gripping it tight. His arm shook slightly but he stood still and straight as he looked up at the pilot.

'Greil,' the pilot said, moving to the near gunwale. 'Feeling a little under the weather?'

'You know. Pressures of the job.' The old man coughed once and grimaced. 'You're still eating well, I see.'

The pilot blinked and smoothed his hands down his flanks. His scalp flushed slightly. 'Pressures of the job,' he said.

The boat rocked. The boy watched the old man's hand on the railing. He could hear how heavily the old man was breathing. He hoped the pilot couldn't hear it.

'Thought I'd better come and check the shipment,' the old man said. He looked down at the water, started to say something else, but his eyes were following a small wave that had come through the open gates and he seemed to lose his train of thought.

'It's all fine,' the boy said.

The old man frowned and looked up. 'Did you bring the spare LEDs this time?'

The corner of the pilot's mouth twitched. 'You know, I believe I did.'

'It's all fine,' the boy said again.

The pilot was watching the old man carefully. 'I've got your items here,' he said. 'Your sticks and stones.'

The old man glanced at the boy, then tipped forward slightly before righting himself.

The pilot bent his head to one side, following the movement. 'No market for it, I'm afraid. But it seems that things turned out for the best, after all, wouldn't you say?'

The old man stared at the pilot. His eyes looked so pale they almost seemed to burn in the dock's dim light. Then his hand loosened on the railing and he slipped sideways. The boy started for the gangway, but the old man managed to grip on and hold himself upright.

The pilot looked on, expressionless.

'Well.' The old man straightened up. 'As ever, this has been a scintillating conversation, but if you'll excuse me, I've got things to do.' He took a deep breath, turned and made his way slowly, but deliberately, back to the stairwell.

The boy and the pilot watched him go. Each footstep echoed back down and around the dock.

'He really does need medicine, doesn't he?' the pilot said.

The boy said nothing.

'Which doesn't put you in a very good trading position, does it? Makes it very hard to be businesslike.'

Still the boy said nothing. He could feel every movement the pilot made through the floor; the adjustments he made to his footing every time a small wave came in.

The pilot looked down at his hands and sighed. 'I want the boat,' he said.

The dock lights buzzed quietly in the gloom.

'What boat?'

The pilot turned to the boy. For a moment, he looked almost sad. 'The boat you came back here on.'

The boy suddenly felt very cold. 'What boat?' he said again.

The pilot let out a long breath through his nose. 'You don't expect me to believe that he actually managed to find you. On a turbine? In the outer fields? He doesn't even know how to use the satnav.'

The boy's mouth felt dry. He turned away and gripped the gunwale. 'You can have anything else.'

'I don't want anything else.'

'You can't have the boat.'

The pilot frowned and shook his head. 'Most unbusiness-like,' he said. 'Most unbusinesslike.'

The pilot steered slowly and carefully through the farm, check-ing his position on the satnav, confirming each of the boy's directions, glancing out of both side windows to make sure he was travelling in the exact centre of the rows.

'So the brave and handsome pilot. The hero of our story …'

The boy stared straight ahead through the windscreen. The blades churned the air into long streaks of cloud.

'… He packed up his boat. Packed it up with …'

226

'You've told that one before,' the boy said. 'He goes out and his boat gets a leak.'

'A leak?'

The boy stayed staring out of the windscreen. The clouds twisted away and were churned again, threading into a thick blanket that spread towards the middle of the farm. If it carried on thickening, then maybe the pilot would get turned around, and not be able to find a way through. But he knew that wouldn't happen. The clouds would lift any minute, gathering together up higher, closing over them like a hatch.

'That's what you said. You said he had a leak and he was taking on water. You said he had a choice between trying to get back and risking sinking, or staying there, bailing, until he was too tired to carry on.'

The pilot frowned. He looked down at the satnav and then back out of the windscreen. 'That doesn't sound right,' he said. 'Our pilot wouldn't be stupid enough to get himself in that situation.'

The waves became darker and choppier. The boy looked out at the turbines they passed. He watched each one, trying to hold it in view for as long as possible, as if that would change things, slow them down; as if it would stop the pilot turning onto a new row and the boy's boat appearing up ahead.

The smell of wax and polish in the cabin was almost overwhelming. The boy kept watching. But it didn't stop anything. There was his boat in the distance, moored to one of the turbines, and the pilot had already seen it and was slowing down.

The boy went out on deck and waited in the bow as the pilot made five attempts to get in close without scratching his paintwork. Eventually, the boy was able to hook onto the gunwale and climb aboard. He stood on his boat for a moment, his feet remembering the particular way it rocked. He watched the bow rise and fall, rise and fall, until there was nothing else he could do except secure the two boats together.

While the pilot checked the knots, the boy crossed to the stern of his boat and looked back at the cabin, at the poles rising up from the deck and the sail, folded neatly, the lines of the rigging and the pulleys angling the ropes to the wheel. There was a dent in the control panel from where his chair had come loose in a gale and been thrown across the cabin. That had been a long and difficult day, but the boat had made it through.

The wind gusted and the poles rattled in their housings. He'd been meaning to fix that.

'Most charming,' the pilot said. He was looking up at the sail, his hands folded on his stomach.

The boy looked up at the sail again. The clouds streamed above it. He rested his hand on the gunwale for a moment, then climbed back onto the supply boat.

'I really am very impressed,' the pilot said, as he followed the satnav back to the rig. 'A mast and sails out of poles and an old tarp. And rigging too. Who would have thought it.'

The boy looked out of the windscreen, keeping his eyes fixed ahead, making sure he couldn't catch sight of his boat in the mirror.

'Your father, I'm sure, would have been very impressed.'

The boy looked round and stared at the pilot, then turned back to the window.

The pilot blinked, checked his coordinates, then cleared his throat. 'So, as I say, the brave and handsome pilot, the hero of our story …' His voice trailed off.

A wave thumped against the supply boat's hull, and a moment later thumped against the hull of the boat being towed behind.

The boy could hear the sound of each wave, the way the white water broke and hissed over the hull. His father had shaped it so that the corners were more rounded than the original – more streamlined. It must have taken weeks, months even, bending over the hull and grinding away layer after layer of metal, then reinforcing it from the inside, polishing it down, making sure the angle was exactly right. Did he ever really think he would get back? The boy would never know. But he'd tried, he'd done what he thought was best, what the boy would probably have done himself. He'd been so young – that's what the boy thought of now. In that small room with the orange chairs, his father had been so young, maybe even younger than the boy was now. He'd shaped the hull so well that the water barely seemed to touch it. The boy pictured each fleck of metal falling away and settling across his boots.

The pilot steered into a new row. A turbine loomed down at them with its crooked blades. The pilot turned back to watch it as they went past. He kept looking at all the warped and broken turbines and his hands twitched on the wheel. He checked the satnav again. They were still a long way out. He pushed on the accelerator. 'What do you think happened?' he said.

'What?'

'To the pilot, bailing out his boat. What do you think happened?'

The boy shook his head. 'It's your bloody story.'

The pilot nodded and breathed deeply. 'Yes, it is. Good point.' His hands flexed on the wheel. 'I think he plugged the leak and he made it home, to a hero's welcome.'

The boy turned and looked at him. 'Do you?'

The pilot blinked. 'I think so.'

The boy watched the pilot closely. There was a tiny bead of sweat above his top lip. Another turbine loomed out in front of them – this one had a hole right through the heart of its tower, which was jagged and blackened, with twists of metal lifting in the wind. Through it, the fields stretched outwards and away, stitching together like a net. The pilot couldn't seem to take his eyes off it.

'You haven't spent a lot of time offshore, have you,' the boy told him.

The two boats made their way slowly into the dock. 'When will you be back with the medicine?' the boy said.

'As soon as I can.' The pilot brought the supply boat to a stop next to the gantry. 'Of course, I'll have to see how much I can get for the boat, but it should do for the first few months' supply.' He cut the engine and turned to face the boy. 'Then we can discuss arrangements for a repeat prescription.'

The boy folded his arms and looked straight into the pilot's eyes. 'And I just have to take your word?'

The pilot pursed his lips. 'We've made a deal. Have I ever gone back on a deal? Have I ever done anything to suggest that …?'

'Okay,' the boy said. 'Okay.'

'In the meantime.' The pilot opened a drawer in the cabinet next to the wheel and brought out a small bottle. 'One a day,' he said. 'Just hope it's not anything resistant.'

The boy came forward and took the bottle. The glass was pale brown and delicate, with a silver cap on the top. The tablets were stacked up inside. They looked like nothing really, just tiny white spheres; small and slightly shiny, no bigger than his fingernail.

'You know,' the pilot said, leaning down and tidying the cabinet, straightening each box and roll of paper. 'If there's ever anything else you want.'

The boy held the bottle carefully, then he put it in his pocket, turned and left the cabin.

'I'm just saying, now that we're on trading terms …'

The boy crossed the deck and was about to lower the gangplank, but then stopped and went back to the cabin.

'Fishing line,' he said from the doorway.

The pilot blinked. 'Excuse me?'

'I want some proper fishing line.'

231

'What for?'

'Fishing.'

The pilot blinked again, nodded, reached into his cabinet drawer and took out a piece of paper and a pencil. 'Fishing line,' he said, writing in small, neat letters. 'For fishing.'

Dust

The boy lay on his bed, listening to the sound of the old man's breathing as it moved through the vents between their rooms. The rig was quiet. There had been strong winds overnight, blowing from the south-east. The boy could tell because they always worked their way up into the waste chute, causing it to emit a low drone. He'd stayed awake listening to it until the early hours, when the wind had dropped.

The air con stuttered and stopped. The filters were probably clogged. He couldn't remember the last time he'd checked them. He couldn't remember the last time he'd checked the maintenance report either. The turbine components he'd stripped for the pilot were still packed in their boxes in the dock. He hadn't sorted the crates from the resupply. The days just seemed to slip quietly past, like currents under the water.

He'd watched the supply boat on the satellite map as it made its way out of the farm, towing his boat behind it. When it passed beyond the map's borders, he'd switched to the weather report. There was a moment when he'd willed there to be a storm, but then he remembered that the pilot had to be alive in order to bring back more medicine.

The old man's breath had turned slow and regular since he'd taken the pills. He slept better, ate and drank a little more. He still coughed, but the fits were fewer, less violent. Sometimes, the boy would hear him get out of bed and walk slowly down the corridor to the toilet. Sometimes, he would hear the scrape of bottles and the rattle of small pieces of plastic. When the boy went to sit with the old man, he tried to explain what had happened to the boat, but he wasn't sure if the old man heard or not, or if he understood; so the boy just cleaned, made the bed, kept the room tidy. He'd put the old man's things back in there – the pins and bones and stones – lining them up with the bottles of plastics, one next to the other.

The boy reached over and picked up one of the technical manuals. He opened it and began to read. He read to the end of the page then stopped, frowned, and read the page again. It was wrong. The instructions it gave for replacing a yaw bearing were in the wrong order. He rested the book on his lap. It said that the radial bearings needed to be inserted after the main bearings, but that wasn't right. The radials were always first, then the main ones after that. He looked down at the page again. Maybe there were more mistakes; maybe everything he'd been reading was wrong, he just hadn't noticed. He folded the cover shut slowly.

It was so quiet he could hear the clock ticking on his wall. He looked over at it. It was ticking, but the second hand wasn't moving at all. He looked back at the ceiling. The clock ticked but didn't move. He got up, pulled the clock from its fixing and threw it into the corner under the sink. The ticking stopped. There was silence. The boy closed his eyes. There was actually silence. No wind, no air con, no sound at all.

He sat up. There was no sound coming from the old man's room. He jumped up from the bed, ran down the corridor to the old man's door and pushed it open. His heart beat loudly in his ears. The old man wasn't there. The boy looked up and down the corridor, then went to the washroom, the toilets, the room where he'd put all the old man's nets and maps. He checked the control room and dock, the transformer level and the galley, his footsteps ringing on the stairs. All of them were empty. He stood in the upper corridor, breathing heavily. Then he noticed a strange light coming from the rec room.

He walked slowly forward and looked in. The room was empty, but steeped in a dusky orange light. It was coming from the window, which was coated in something and impossible to see through. He crossed the room and cupped his eyes against the glass, but couldn't make out anything beyond it.

There was no sound of the wind or the sea. There was nothing. He remembered, for a terrifying moment, what it had been like to be completely alone on the outer turbine. The walls seemed to press in. There wasn't enough air. What had the pilot said? The old man had waited a year before he finally admitted that the boy's father had gone.

There were footsteps coming from above his head. He left the rec room and went to the hatch that led out to the roof.

He stopped and listened, heard nothing. He turned the handle, pushed and almost fell through the opening – there was no resistance from the wind.

He stumbled out and squinted against the strange red glow that seemed to emanate from every surface. Everything was totally still – the blades, the sea, the sky. The boy blinked and waited for his eyes to adjust, because everything still seemed red. He blinked again, pressed his knuckles into his eyes, but the red was still there, covering the rig, the towers, the blades, even the edges of the clouds and the surface of the sea. It was as if another place had laid itself down when he wasn't looking, silently, pressing into every edge and corner.

There were footprints leading from the hatch out to the cracked helipad. The boy crouched down and ran his finger along the metal. It was dust. He stood up and turned around. The whole farm, as far as he could see, was coated in a layer of dust.

He followed the line of footprints, making his own, slowly and deliberately next to them, watching how the dust compressed to form a perfect outline of his boot-tread. As he walked, he ran his palm along the rail and gathered up almost a handful, which he held and poured from one hand to the other, watching how it clung to his skin, gathering in the cracks and creases, highlighting the wave-like patterns of his fingerprints. It was gritty and light, almost soft. He rubbed his hands together and the dust rose up into the air.

The old man was standing in the centre of the helipad. He had shaved, leaving a few lines of grey stubble in the creases of his neck. His hair too was flecked with grey, but his eyes were less dull and his jaw had lost its tension. The boy went over and stood next to him.

'Comes from the desert,' the old man said eventually.

'The desert?'

'You know what that is?'

The boy looked down at the dust. 'Somewhere dusty.'

The old man glanced over at the boy. 'Dusty and hot.'

The boy nodded, crouched down and laid his palm on the roof of the rig. It seemed warm, but that could have been because they were standing over the heating system.

'Nights get cold, though,' the old man continued. 'So cold you could freeze in your bed.'

'Like here then?'

'But not wet.' The old man closed his eyes. 'In the desert there's no water at all.'

The boy looked out at the sea. The dust had coated the surface so that it didn't look like water any more. It looked almost solid, as if they could just step down there and walk towards the horizon. The more the boy looked, the more it seemed like he could do it; he could almost imagine the feeling of it under his feet, how firm it would be, how unmoving. Then a small wave surged in and broke the layer of dust, crumbling the edges. A moment later, it settled back to stillness.

'It used to be like that here,' the old man said.

'Desert?'

'Land.'

'I know.'

'All of this, as far as we can see, would have been land.'

'I know.'

The old man bent down and picked up a pinch of dust. 'Everything changes, if you wait long enough.'

The boy stood up and brushed the dust off his hands. 'I don't want to wait.'

The old man carried on looking out to sea.

'We can make another boat,' the boy said. 'Better than the last one. There are things here we can use. And things always drift through. All we need are tarps, poles, some rope.' He'd spent a long time thinking about exactly what they would need, working out whether anything they already had on the rig could be used. The sheets off the bed would be too flimsy and would tear in the first gale. The old man's poles would buckle. Everything he thought of he had to dismiss, until there was only the option of waiting, watching the water, seeing what might come in.

The old man ground the pinch of dust slowly between his fingers. 'That's all going to drift through, is it?'

'Well, where did he get it from before?'

The old man frowned. 'I don't remember.'

'What about the batteries?'

'They were the spares.'

'And you just let him take them?'

The old man kept his eyes fixed on the horizon. 'He said he needed them.' The dust had settled in a fine line over his eyelashes.

The boy bent down and ran his fingers in the dust again. The grains banked up under his nails.

'Do you remember him?' the old man said.

The boy stared down at his hand – there were so many grains under his nails, millions probably, if he could count them all. 'Not much,' he said.

The old man nodded. 'But you thought about him.'

The boy reached up and rubbed the side of his jaw, then dropped his hand back down.

'I mean … did you …' The old man stopped and cleared his throat. He squinted out at the strange brightness. 'It'll be calm now,' he said. 'For a few days.'

The boy turned and looked at the old man. 'It won't happen to us.'

The old man carried on looking at the sky. 'Have you drawn up the schedule for tomorrow yet? We've got behind.'

'What happened to him,' the boy said. 'It won't happen to us. I managed the boat all the way through the farm. With both of us …'

'There won't be both of us.'

'What?'

The old man took a rattly breath and coughed, but the coughing stopped almost as soon as it had started. 'I'll help you get the boat ready, if the right stuff comes through, but you'll have to sail it yourself.'

'But you're getting better. The pilot …'

'It's not about that.' The old man breathed out slowly.

For a moment the dust seemed too thick, too dry. The boy could feel it on his eyelids, between his teeth. 'So you're giving up?'

The old man sighed again, took one more look across the farm then turned and made his way back towards the hatch.

The boy followed him. 'You're just going to stay here? Doing what? Trawling up junk? A room full of tiny bits of plastic? Sitting on your own, thinking about a place that doesn't even exist any more?'

The old man stopped. 'I have to.'

'Why?'

'Because I'm on a contract,' he said quietly. 'Same contract your father was on. He left and you ended up out here. If I leave …' He looked out at the water, past the water. His jaw was tight again.

The boy stood very still. He looked over at the two sets of footprints leading back towards the hatch. As they got further away, it was hard to tell whose were whose.

The old man wiped the dust off his hands, watching as the flecks dropped to the ground. 'Let me know the schedule for tomorrow,' he said. He carried on to the hatch, then turned back. 'He was just like you,' he said. 'Always bloody fixing things. Did I ever tell you that?'

The boy watched the old man go. Then he called out, 'Greil?'

The old man was about to duck through the hatch but he stopped and waited.

'I did think of him,' the boy said. 'I still do.'

The old man nodded. His hand gripped the railing. His skin was coated with dust, except in the lines where he was holding hard to the metal.

Then, slowly, his hand relaxed. After a moment he turned

round and straightened up. Then he popped his knuckles softly, savouring each crack. A small cloud of dust floated across the rig in the wind.

'System crashed again this morning,' the old man said.

'What did you do?' the boy said.

The old man shrugged. 'I didn't do anything. It just crashed. Then when it rebooted all the screens were green.'

'Green?'

'All of them.'

The boy brushed the dust off his overalls. 'Why green?' he said.

'How am I meant to know?'

'That doesn't sound good.'

'Well, what would you prefer, blue?' the old man said.

'What?'

'The screens. When they crash.'

'I'd prefer it if they didn't crash,' the boy said.

'What if you had to pick a colour?'

'Why would I have to pick a colour?'

'Jesus, just pick a colour.'

'Black.'

'You're picking black?'

'You said to pick a colour.'

'And you picked black.'

'What?'

'Jesus,' the old man said again. He shook his head, then went back into the rig, muttering something about the boy having no imagination.

The boy looked back out across the farm. Gradually, the wind picked up, the clouds began to push back in and the dust was slowly scoured away, leaving just the thinnest threads caught in the rivet-lines and crevices of the metal.

At least he knew what it was that had shut down the air con. He could look forward to a long night scrubbing out all the dust from the filters.

Slowly, starting from the west, the blades began to turn. Almost all of the turbines near to the rig were still. The boy thought of the components down in the dock. He could put them back where he'd found them, but maybe it would be better to save them out and see where they were most needed. He'd forget about the maintenance report – the next day he and the old man would start early, pick an area and go and check all the turbines themselves. There would be gearboxes to grease, blade controls to reset and rewire. He'd been wanting to have a go at overhauling a generator for a long time. In the right conditions, they could get through fifteen, maybe twenty a day. The farm had over six thousand turbines, which meant they could get round them all in three to four hundred days. Of course, that didn't take into account the lack of spare parts, the weeks when the weather kept them stuck on the rig, or the fact that they would have to save out the best components to trade with the pilot. It didn't take into account the cracks and draughts and drips on the rig that would need to be reinforced, sealed, shored-up, just to keep it all from crumbling into the sea. Or the fact that, whenever the boy said a bearing needed replacing, the old man would argue and say it probably didn't, and then he would bet the boy a tin of protein on it, and they would have to check, and when the boy was inevitably right, the old man would say they had to check again. Or the fact that, when they were on their way to the next job, they could just as easily end up sorting through one of the old man's nets.

But they had a lot of time on their hands.

The boy looked up at the sky. There was perhaps a slightly paler patch of cloud out towards the west. There was a lot of the day still left. He didn't go straight back to the service hatch, but climbed down the ladder to the platform at the bottom of the south-west support. Out in the fields, the blades were turning faster, working up into a steady rhythm. The wind droned through the grilles. Thirteen metres per second. The farm would generate well today.

He squatted down and took hold of his line. The water was murky, clouded with the last of the dust, but he could see some way. Who knew what he might find? After all, this was once a whole country, a whole continent.

Fourth hook down he noticed something.

'Strange fish,' he said, his voice merging with the wind.

Year Zero

And now it is just water. Or, not quite just water.

At some point, blocks were laid down to stabilize the seabed. Posts and rods were driven in. Metal was stacked on metal. Towers rose from the water like the trunks of long-forgotten trees.

The trees grew branches. The wind blew and the branches turned. The wind blew and the branches thrummed and turned. Cables spread like roots. Energy gathered and spread.

When did this happen? Maybe centuries ago. Nothing more than a blink in the lifetime of water.

But they are here. And so, water continues its work – of levelling, of pressing at edges, of constantly seeking a return to an even surface, a steady state. It repeats its mantra: solidity is nothing but an interruption to continuous flow, an obstacle to be overcome, an imbalance to be rectified.

It finds its way through cracks and rivets. It scrapes away metal, millimetre by millimetre. It chips paint and crumbles rubber seals. It finds new ways to make things bloom.

Sometimes, it finds its work undone. A crack is filled, a panel is reinforced. But the water is patient. It's been doing this for a long time.

The wind blows, the branches creak and turn. Somewhere in the metal forest, a tree slumps, groans, but does not quite fall.

The landscape holds fast, for a moment.

For how long? It may be centuries. Barely worth mentioning in the lifetime of water.

Acknowledgements

Thank you to my agent Euan Thorneycroft and my editor Helen Garnons-Williams for their wonderful advice, enthusiasm and faith in the novel; to the teams at A. M. Heath and 4th Estate; to Jos Smith, Sam North and Emma Bird for reading early drafts and giving invaluable advice and encouragement; to Nan-Jui (Mike) Chen for his help with the Chinese translations (any mistakes are entirely my own); to the Roger and Laura Farnworth Residency at Warleggan, which gave me two weeks to write in quiet and beautiful surroundings; to my colleagues in the English and Creative Writing Department at the University of Plymouth for creating an inspiring and supportive environment in which to work; and to Andy Brown, Sam North and Philip Hensher for teaching me how to write. Thank you to my family and friends for their support and encouragement. Thank you to Lucy, for everything.

The following books and articles were very helpful when researching the history, geography and archaeology of Doggerland:

B.J. Coles, 'Doggerland: A Speculative Survey', *Proceedings of the Prehistoric Society*, Volume 64, January 1998.

Vincent Gaffney, Simon Fitch and David Smith, *Europe's Lost World: The Rediscovery of Doggerland*, Research Report No. 160, Council for British Archaeology, 2009.

Nicholas Crane, *The Making of the British Landscape: From the Ice Age to the Present*, Weidenfeld & Nicolson, 2016.

Brian Fagan, *The Attacking Ocean: The Past, Present and Future of Rising Sea Levels*, Bloomsbury Press, 2013.

Steven Mithen, *After the Ice: A Global History of Humanity, 20,000–5000 BC*, Weidenfeld & Nicolson, 2003.